TRANSFORMERS

ANIMATED

VOLUME 9

GARBAGE IN, GARBAGE OUT
WRITTEN BY:
MARTY ISENBERG

VELOCITY
WRITTEN BY:
LEN UHLEY

ADAPTATION BY:
ZACHARY RAU

EDITS BY:
JUSTIN EISINGER

LETTERS AND DESIGN BY:
TOM B. LONG

ISBN: 978-1-60010-435-0
12 11 10 9 1 2 3 4 5

Licensed by:

Hasbro

IDW

Special thanks to Hasbro's Aaron Archer, Michael Kelly,
Amie Lozanski, Val Roca, Ed Lane, Michael Provost,
Erin Hillman, Samantha Lomow, and Michael Verrecchia
for their invaluable assistance.

IDW Publishing is:
Operations:
Ted Adams, Chief Executive Officer
Greg Goldstein, Chief Operating Officer
Matthew Ruzicka, CPA, Chief Financial Officer
Alan Payne, VP of Sales

Lorelei Bunjes, Dir. of Digital Services
AnnaMaria White, Marketing & PR Manager
Marci Hubbard, Executive Assistant
Alonzo Simon, Shipping Manager

Editorial:
Chris Ryall, Publisher/Editor-in-Chief
Scott Dunbier, Editor, Special Projects
Andy Schmidt, Senior Editor
Justin Eisinger, Editor

Kris Oprisko, Editor/Foreign Lic.
Denton J. Tipton, Editor
Tom Waltz, Editor
Mariah Huehner, Associate Editor

Design:
Robbie Robbins, EVP/Sr. Graphic Artist
Ben Templesmith, Artist/Designer
Neil Uyetake, Art Director

Chris Mowry, Graphic Artist
Amauri Osorio, Graphic Artist
Gilberto Lazcano, Production Assistant

To discuss this issue of *Transformers*, or join
the IDW Insiders, or to check out exclusive Web
offers, check out our site:

www.IDWPUBLISHING.com

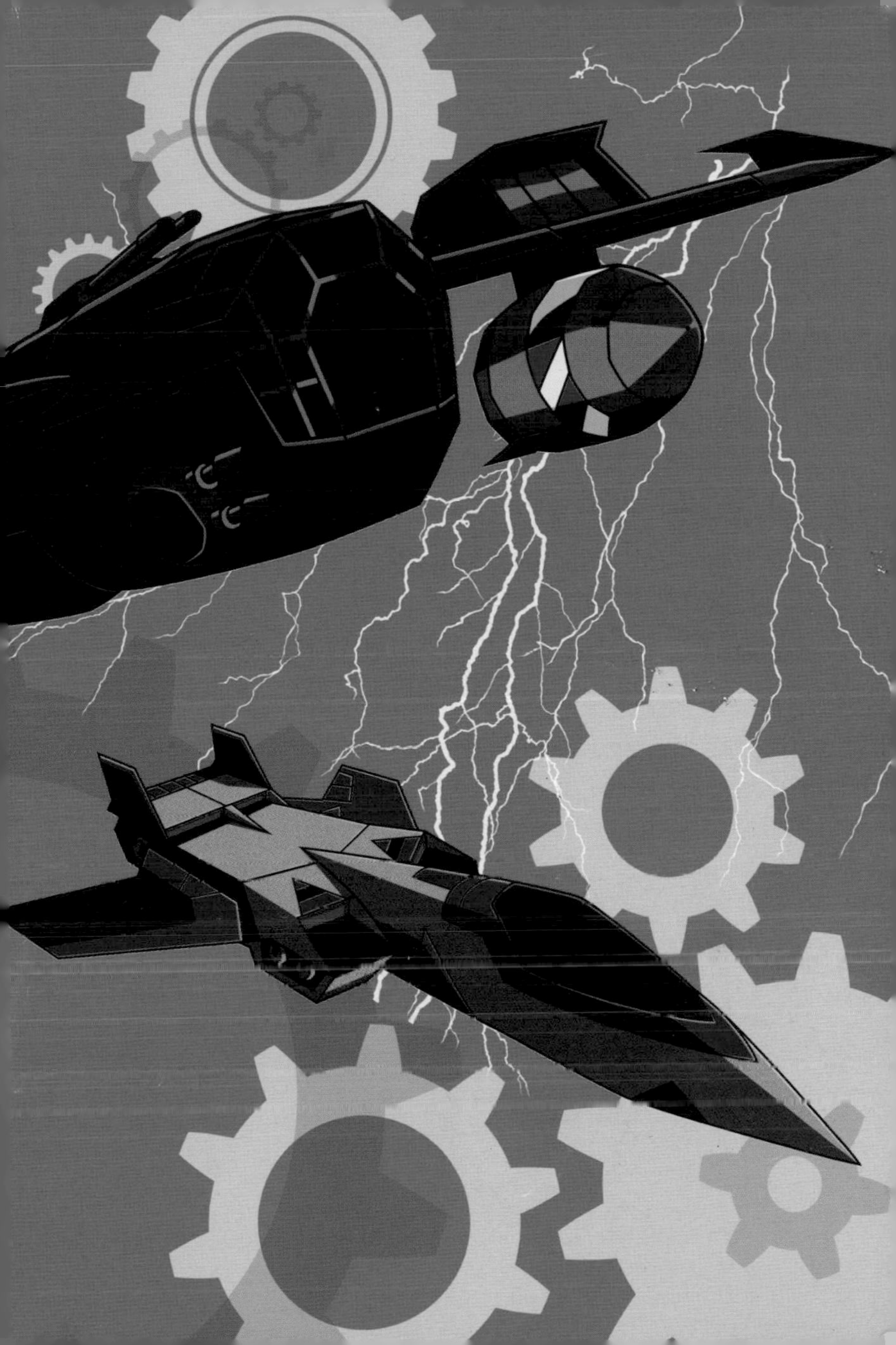

Roll Call

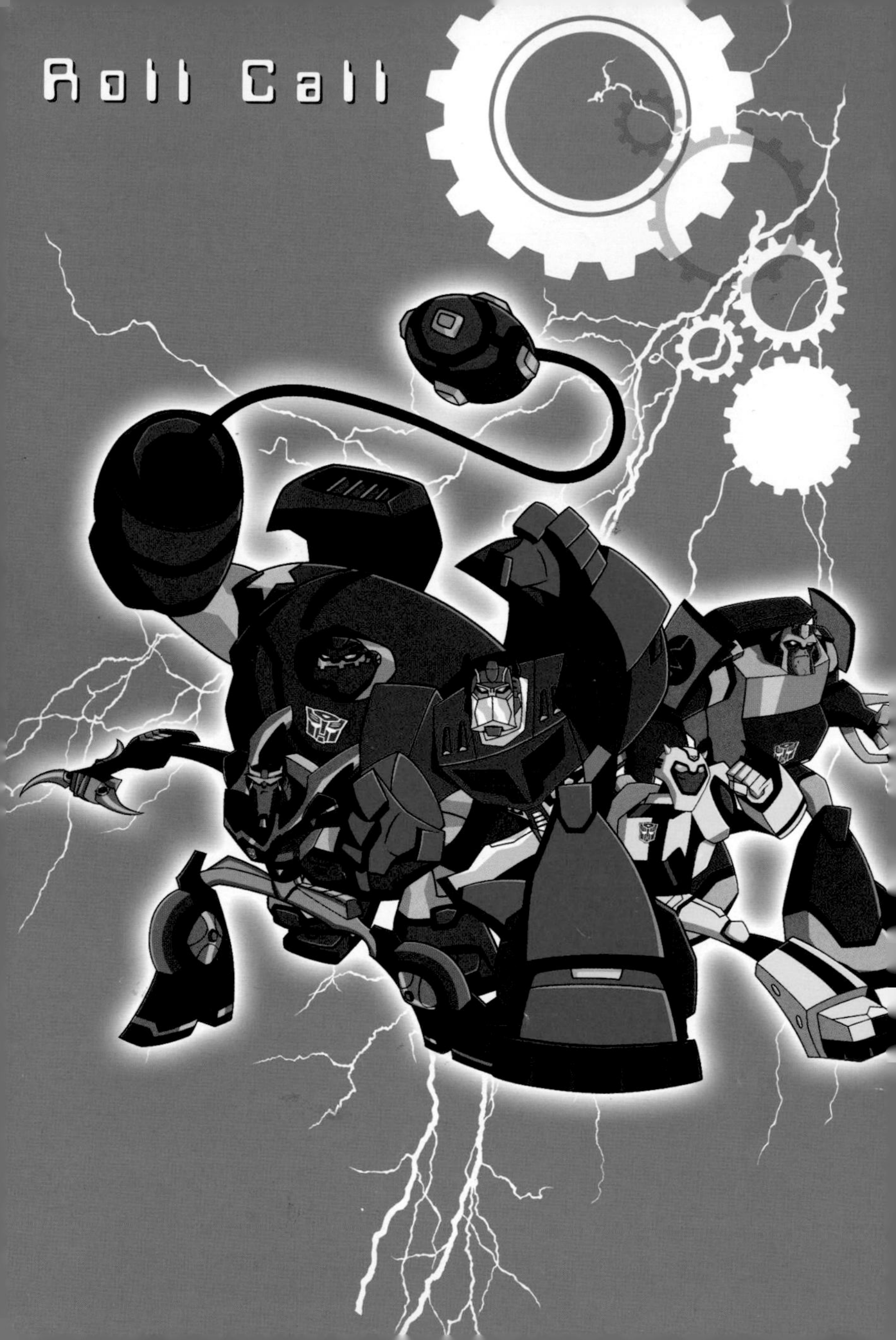

Optimus Prime

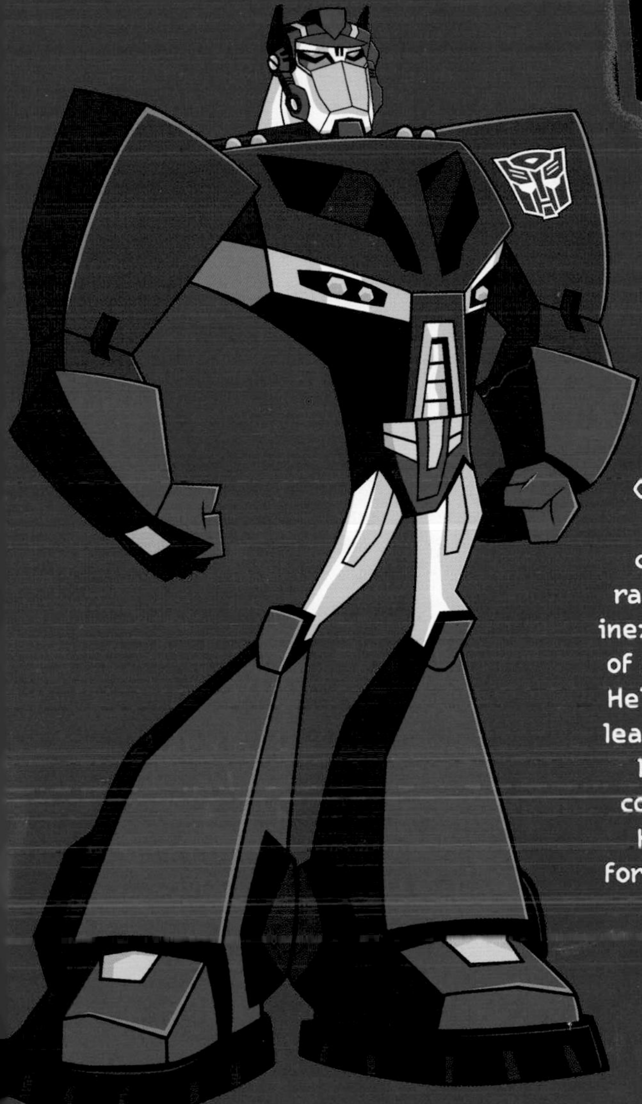

OPTIMUS PRIME is the young commander of a ragtag and largely inexperienced group of misfit AUTOBOTS. He's not the kind of leader who needs to bark orders to command respect. His mechanized form is a fire truck.

Ratchet

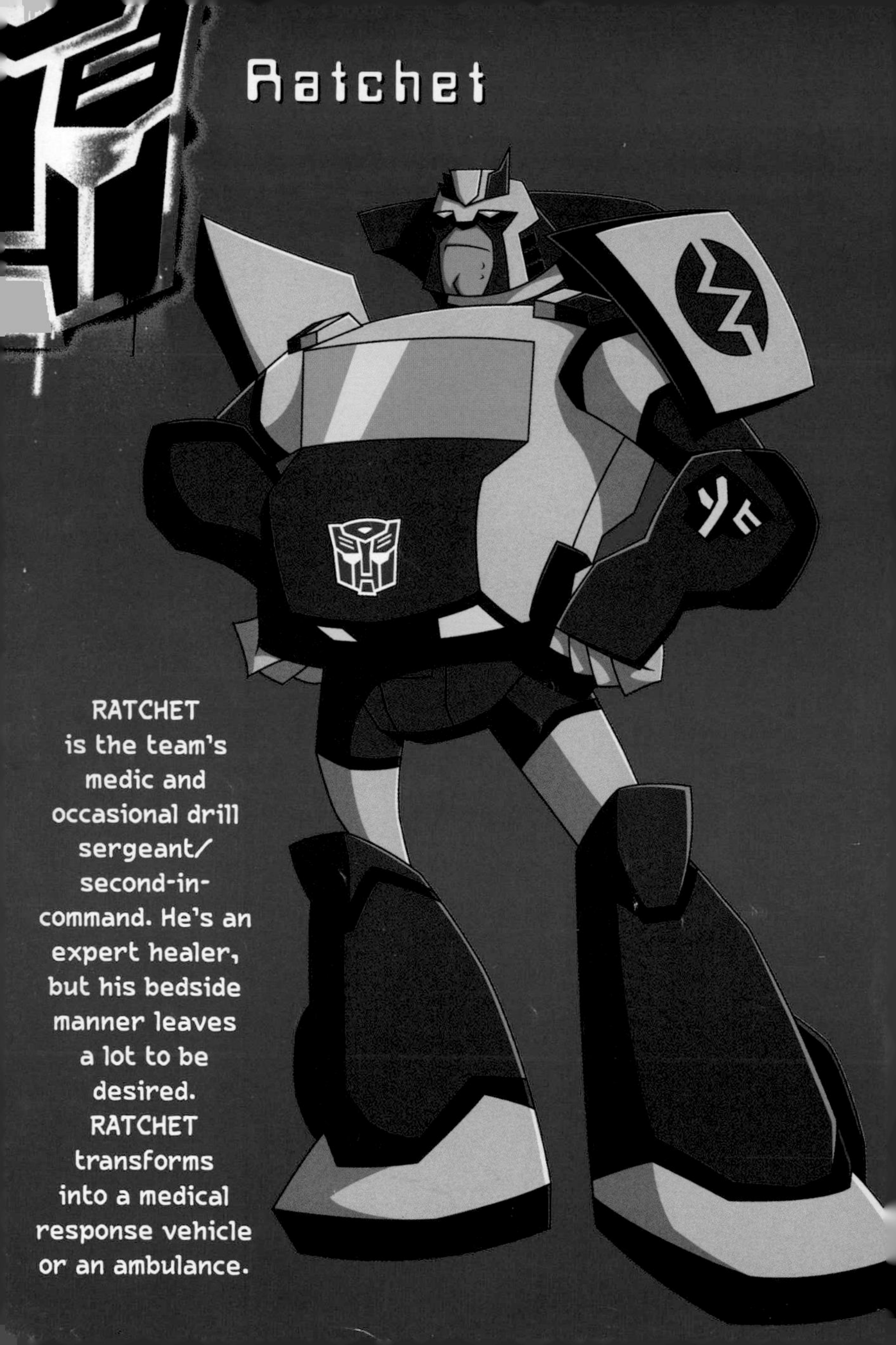

RATCHET is the team's medic and occasional drill sergeant/second-in-command. He's an expert healer, but his bedside manner leaves a lot to be desired. RATCHET transforms into a medical response vehicle or an ambulance.

Bulkhead

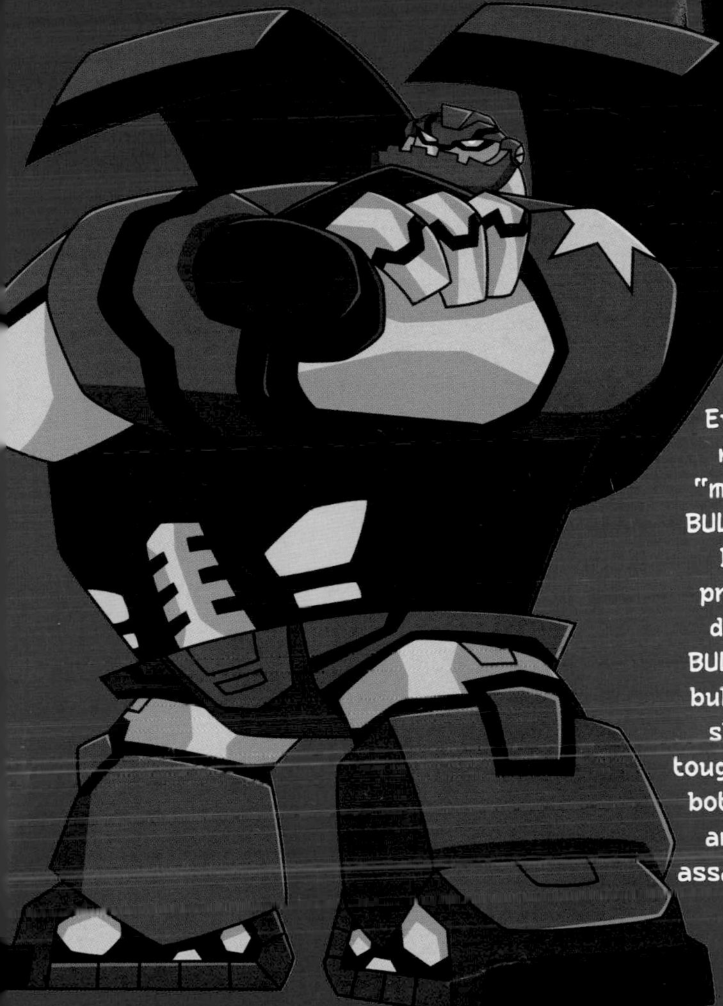

Every team needs its "muscle" and BULKHEAD is it. Designed primarily for demolition, BULKHEAD is a bull in a china shop. He is tough as nails in both his robot and S.W.A.T. assault cruiser forms.

Bumblebee

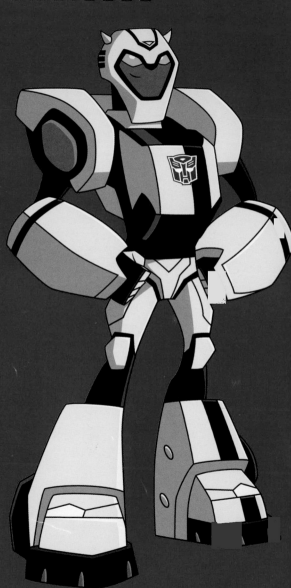

BUMBLEBEE is the "kid" of the team, easily the youngest and least mature of the AUTOBOTS. He's a bit of a showoff, always acting on impulse and rarely considering the consequences. But, he looks awesome in his undercover police cruiser form.

Prowl

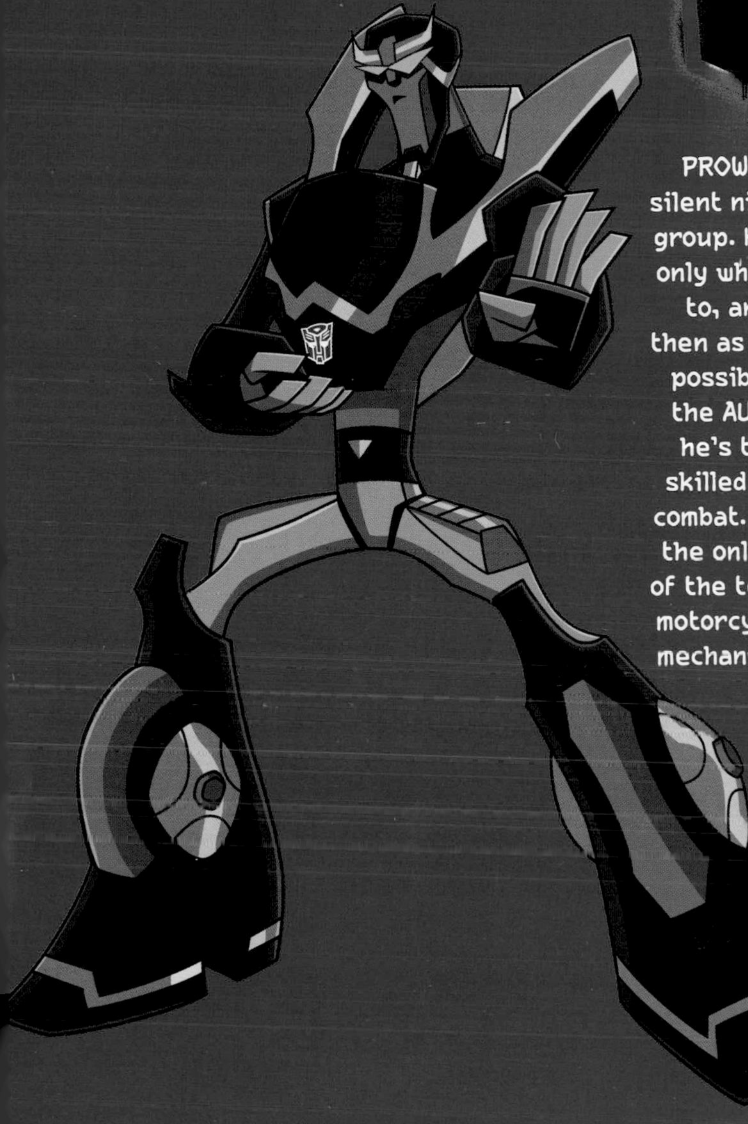

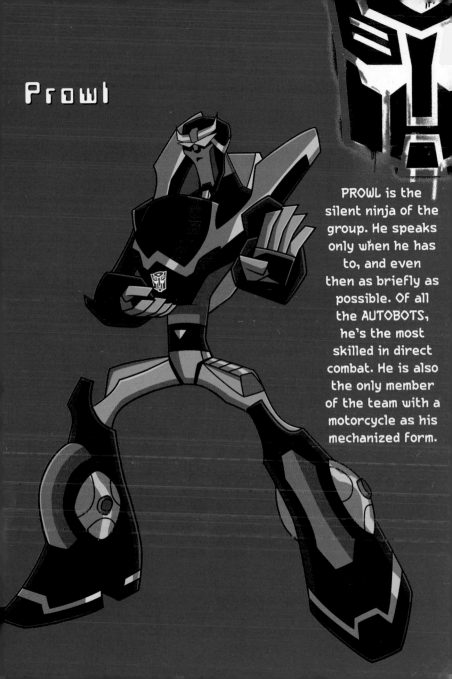

PROWL is the silent ninja of the group. He speaks only when he has to, and even then as briefly as possible. Of all the AUTOBOTS, he's the most skilled in direct combat. He is also the only member of the team with a motorcycle as his mechanized form.

Sari

SARI is the adopted
daughter of Professor Sumdac.
Call it an accident or call it
destiny, but the AllSpark
projected part of itself onto
her in the form of a key.
Wearing it on a chain around
her neck, SARI can use the key
to absorb the AllSpark energy
and store it like a battery,
providing an emergency power
supply and healing source for
the AUTOBOTS in battle. It also
provides her with an almost
psychic connection to
the AUTOBOTS.

Captain Fanzone

CAPTAIN FANZONE is not an AUTOBOT, but a police detective whose car was scanned to become the vehicle mode for BUMBLEBEE. He's a harried, overworked, but basically good and honest cop, albeit one whose day is perpetually ruined by one of those "giant walking toasters."

Porter C. Powell

Porter C. Powell is a very rich and influential businessman who is on the board of directors of Sumdac Systems. He is next in line to take over Sumdac Industries.

Megatron

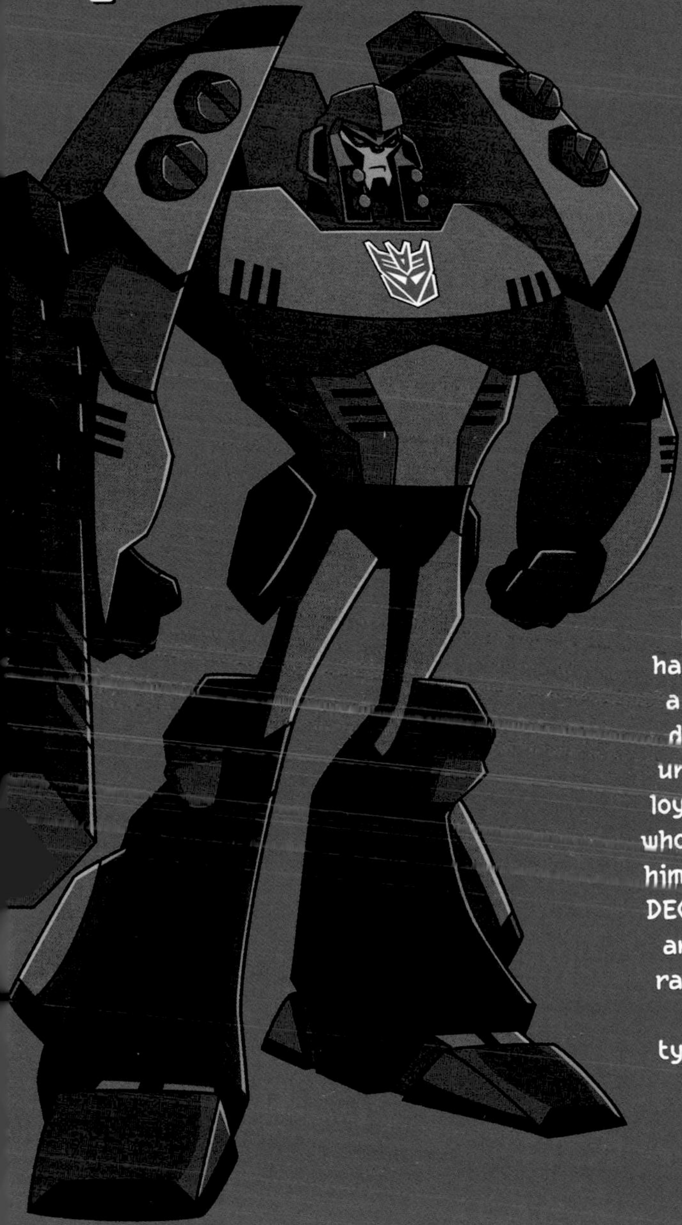

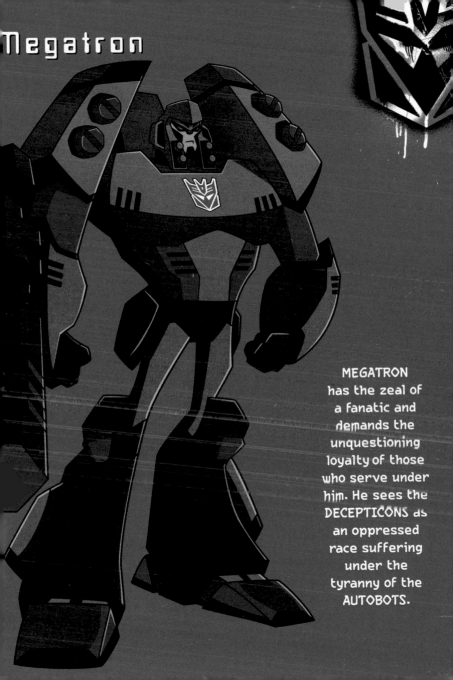

MEGATRON has the zeal of a fanatic and demands the unquestioning loyalty of those who serve under him. He sees the DECEPTICONS as an oppressed race suffering under the tyranny of the AUTOBOTS.

Blitzwing

BLITZWING is
the joker of the
DECEPTICONS.
An unpredictable
multiple personality
bot, he is driven mad
by his constantly
shifting appearance.
BLITZWING is a
"triple-changer"...
that is, he has three
modes (one robot,
two vehicles). Plus
he has three faces,
each with its own
personality. His
power depends
on which face
he's showing:
heat/flame,
cold/ice, or
completely
random.

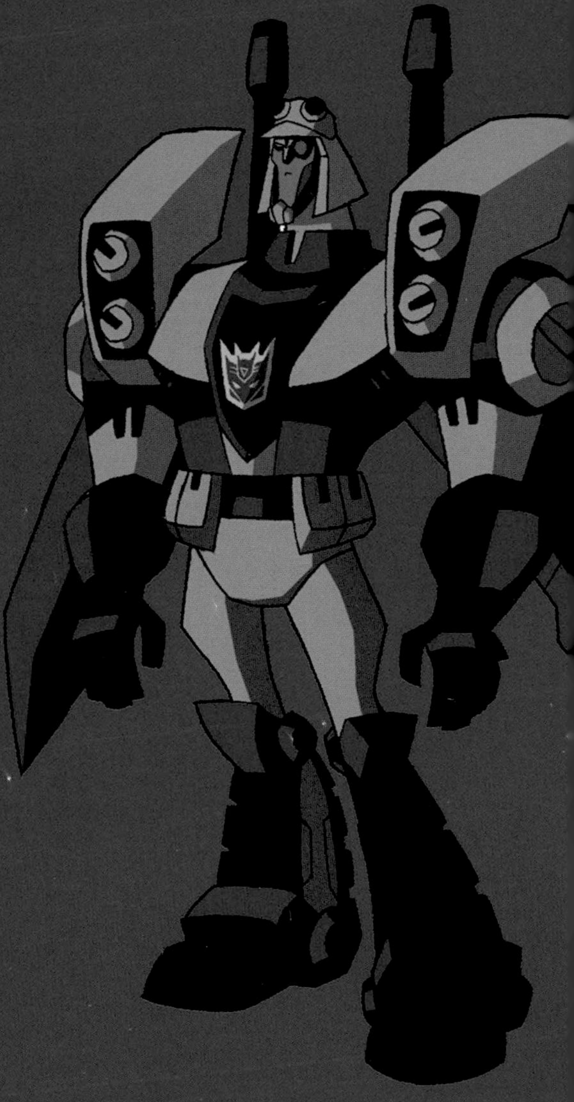

Lugnut

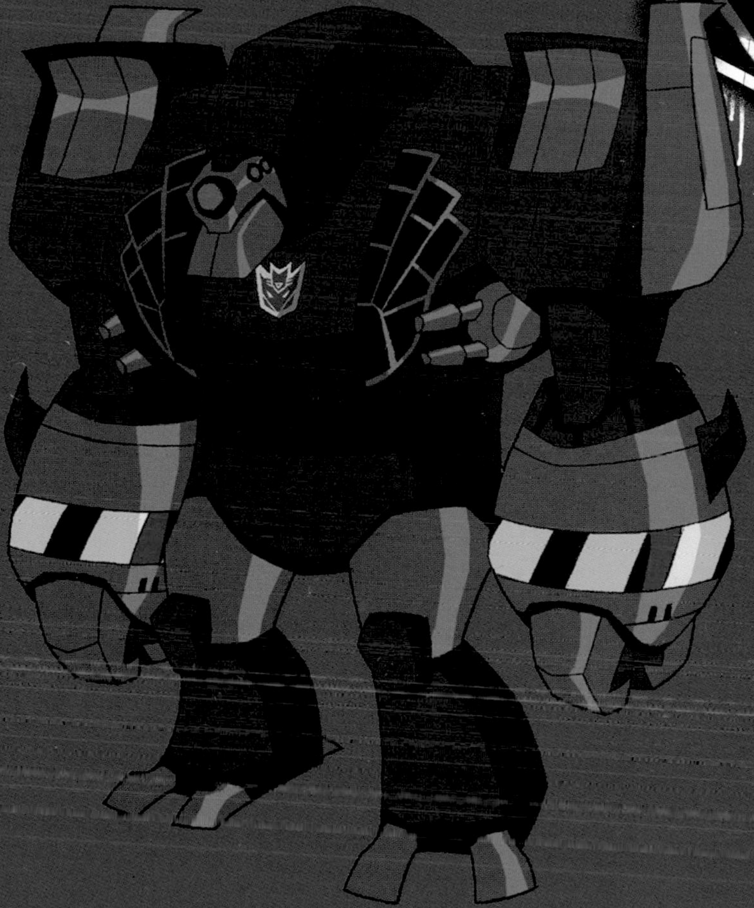

LUGNUT is more a force of nature than a DECEPTICON. MEGATRON's fiercely loyal, but none-too-bright attack dog, he would gladly follow his leader into any battle. Incredibly strong, LUGNUT carries a payload of mega-bombs, and can spew liquid napalm with laser-like accuracy, but he prefers to rip things apart with his bare hands.

GARBAGE IN, GARBAGE OUT

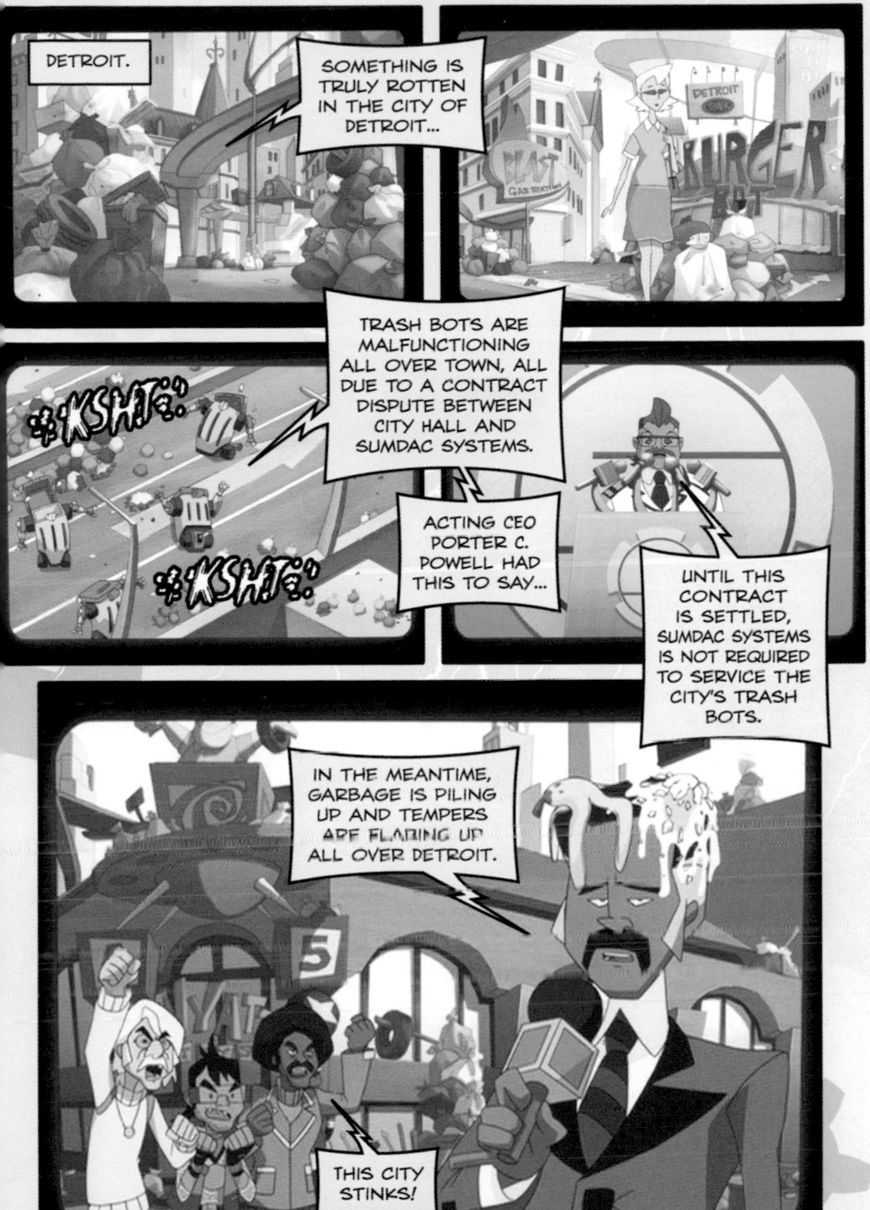
DETROIT.
SOMETHING IS TRULY ROTTEN IN THE CITY OF DETROIT...
TRASH BOTS ARE MALFUNCTIONING ALL OVER TOWN, ALL DUE TO A CONTRACT DISPUTE BETWEEN CITY HALL AND SUMDAC SYSTEMS.
KSHT
KSHT
ACTING CEO PORTER C. POWELL HAD THIS TO SAY...
UNTIL THIS CONTRACT IS SETTLED, SUMDAC SYSTEMS IS NOT REQUIRED TO SERVICE THE CITY'S TRASH BOTS.
IN THE MEANTIME, GARBAGE IS PILING UP AND TEMPERS ARE FLARING UP ALL OVER DETROIT.
THIS CITY STINKS!

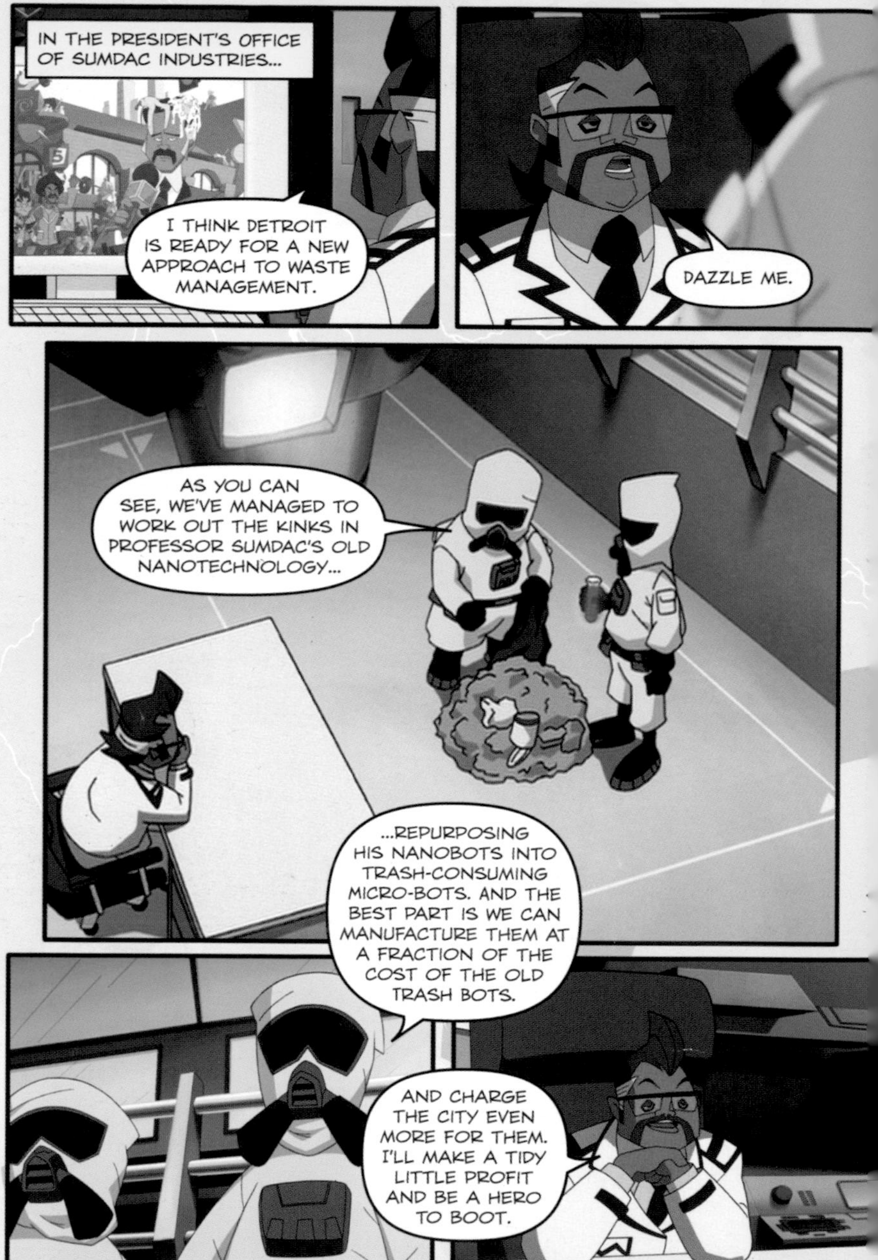
IN THE PRESIDENT'S OFFICE OF SUMDAC INDUSTRIES...
I THINK DETROIT IS READY FOR A NEW APPROACH TO WASTE MANAGEMENT.
DAZZLE ME.
AS YOU CAN SEE, WE'VE MANAGED TO WORK OUT THE KINKS IN PROFESSOR SUMDAC'S OLD NANOTECHNOLOGY...
...REPURPOSING HIS NANOBOTS INTO TRASH-CONSUMING MICRO-BOTS. AND THE BEST PART IS WE CAN MANUFACTURE THEM AT A FRACTION OF THE COST OF THE OLD TRASH BOTS.
AND CHARGE THE CITY EVEN MORE FOR THEM. I'LL MAKE A TIDY LITTLE PROFIT AND BE A HERO TO BOOT.

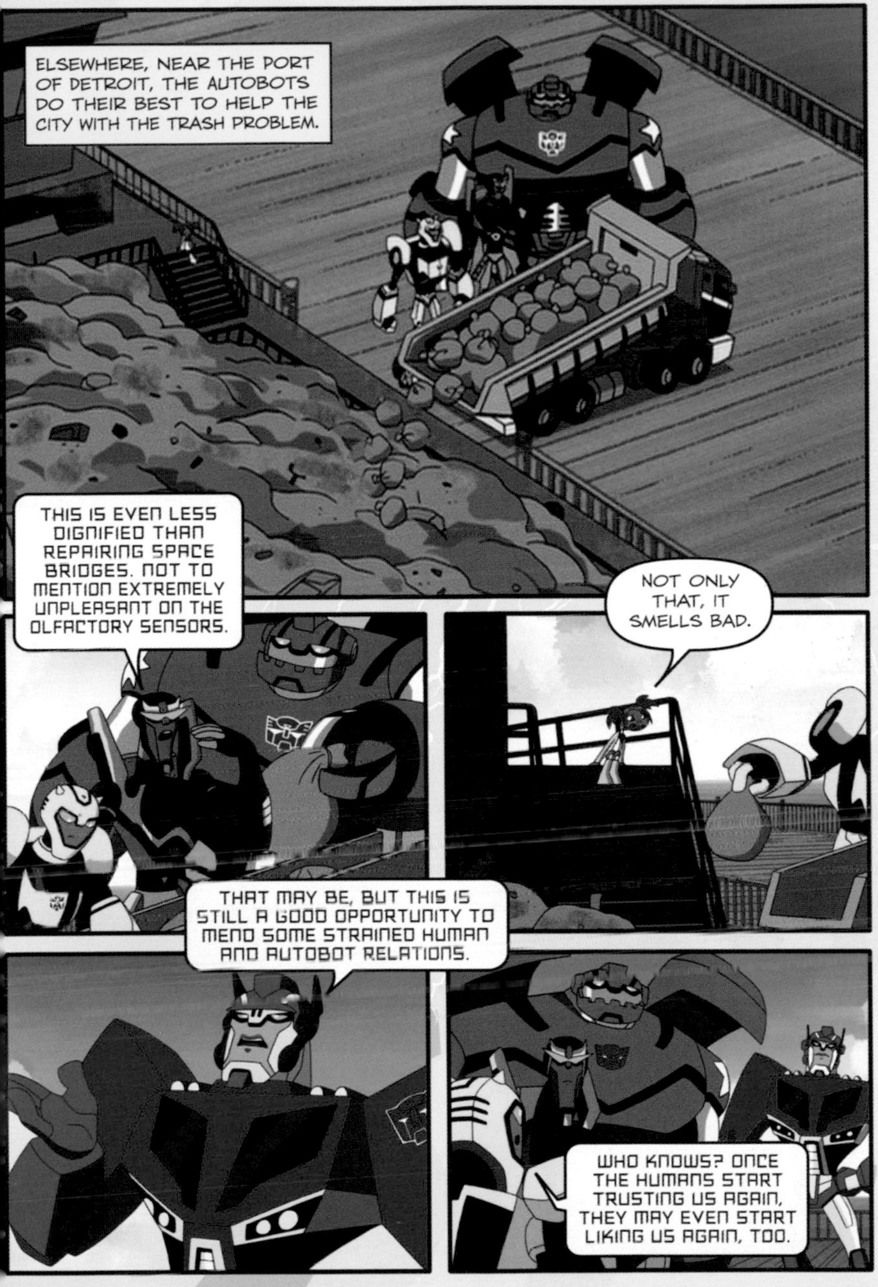
ELSEWHERE, NEAR THE PORT OF DETROIT, THE AUTOBOTS DO THEIR BEST TO HELP THE CITY WITH THE TRASH PROBLEM.
THIS IS EVEN LESS DIGNIFIED THAN REPAIRING SPACE BRIDGES. NOT TO MENTION EXTREMELY UNPLEASANT ON THE OLFACTORY SENSORS.
NOT ONLY THAT, IT SMELLS BAD.
THAT MAY BE, BUT THIS IS STILL A GOOD OPPORTUNITY TO MEND SOME STRAINED HUMAN AND AUTOBOT RELATIONS.
WHO KNOWS? ONCE THE HUMANS START TRUSTING US AGAIN, THEY MAY EVEN START LIKING US AGAIN, TOO.

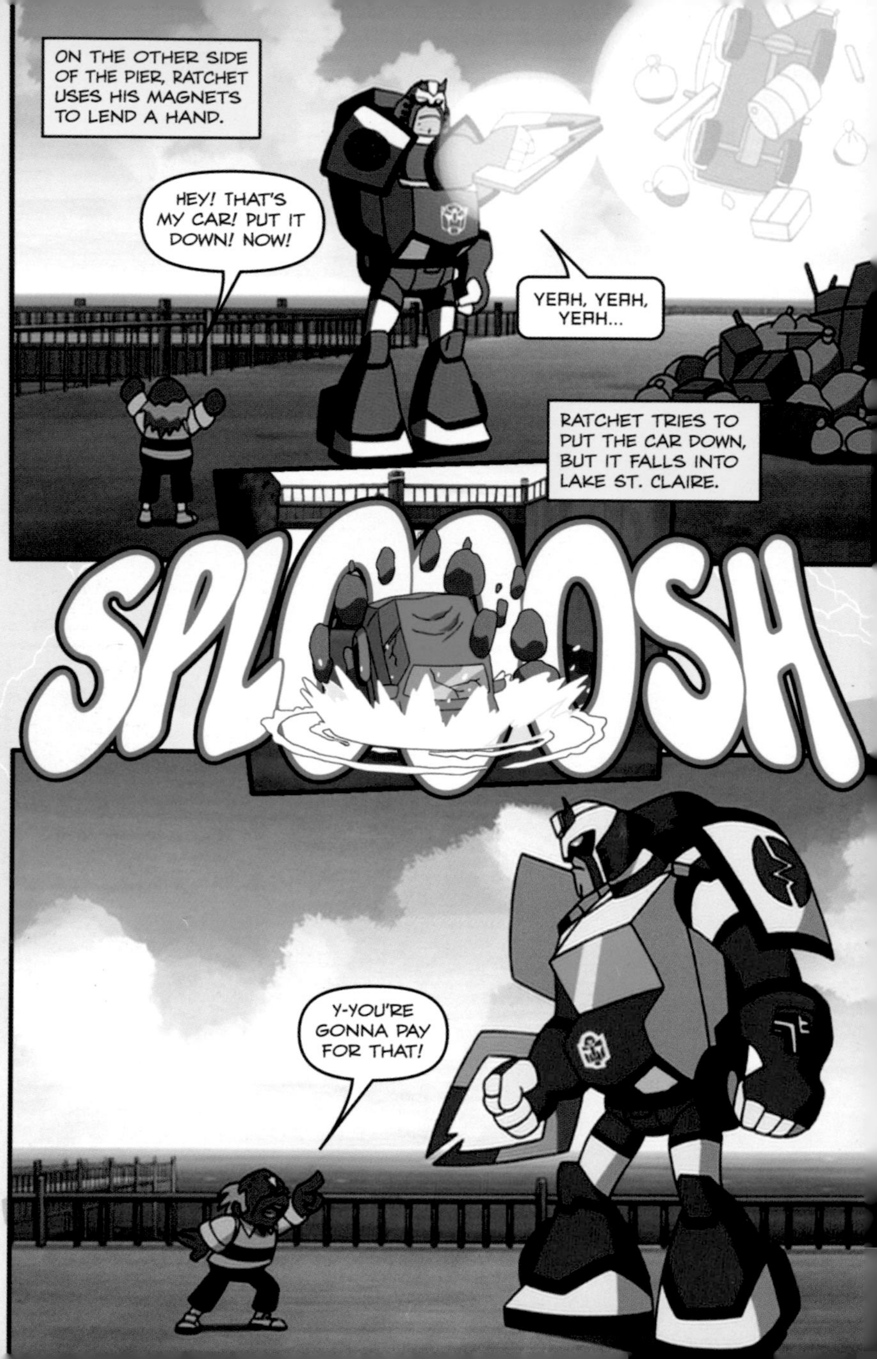
ON THE OTHER SIDE OF THE PIER, RATCHET USES HIS MAGNETS TO LEND A HAND.
HEY! THAT'S MY CAR! PUT IT DOWN! NOW!
YEAH, YEAH, YEAH...
RATCHET TRIES TO PUT THE CAR DOWN, BUT IT FALLS INTO LAKE ST. CLAIRE.
SPLOOOSH
Y-YOU'RE GONNA PAY FOR THAT!

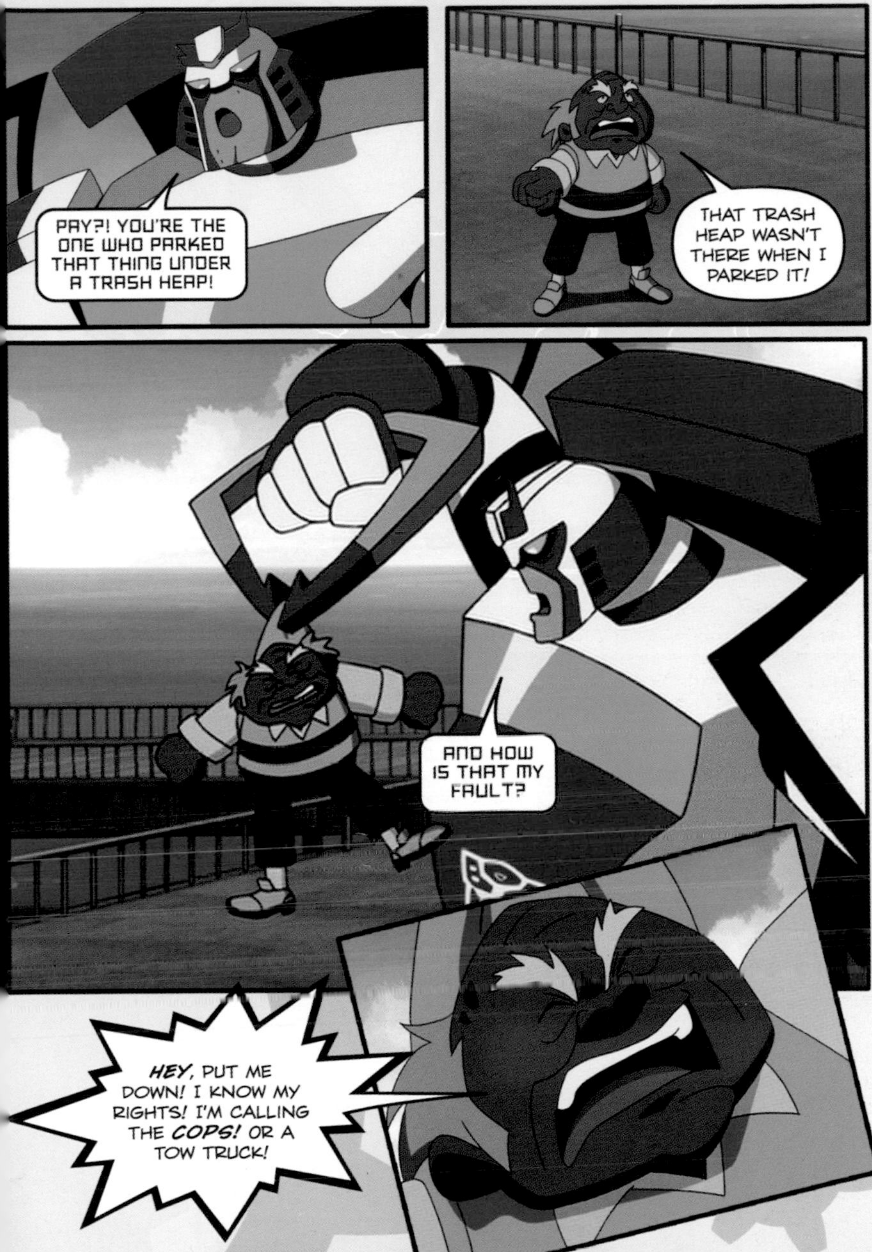
PAY?! YOU'RE THE ONE WHO PARKED THAT THING UNDER A TRASH HEAP!
THAT TRASH HEAP WASN'T THERE WHEN I PARKED IT!
AND HOW IS THAT MY FAULT?
HEY, PUT ME DOWN! I KNOW MY RIGHTS! I'M CALLING THE COPS! OR A TOW TRUCK!

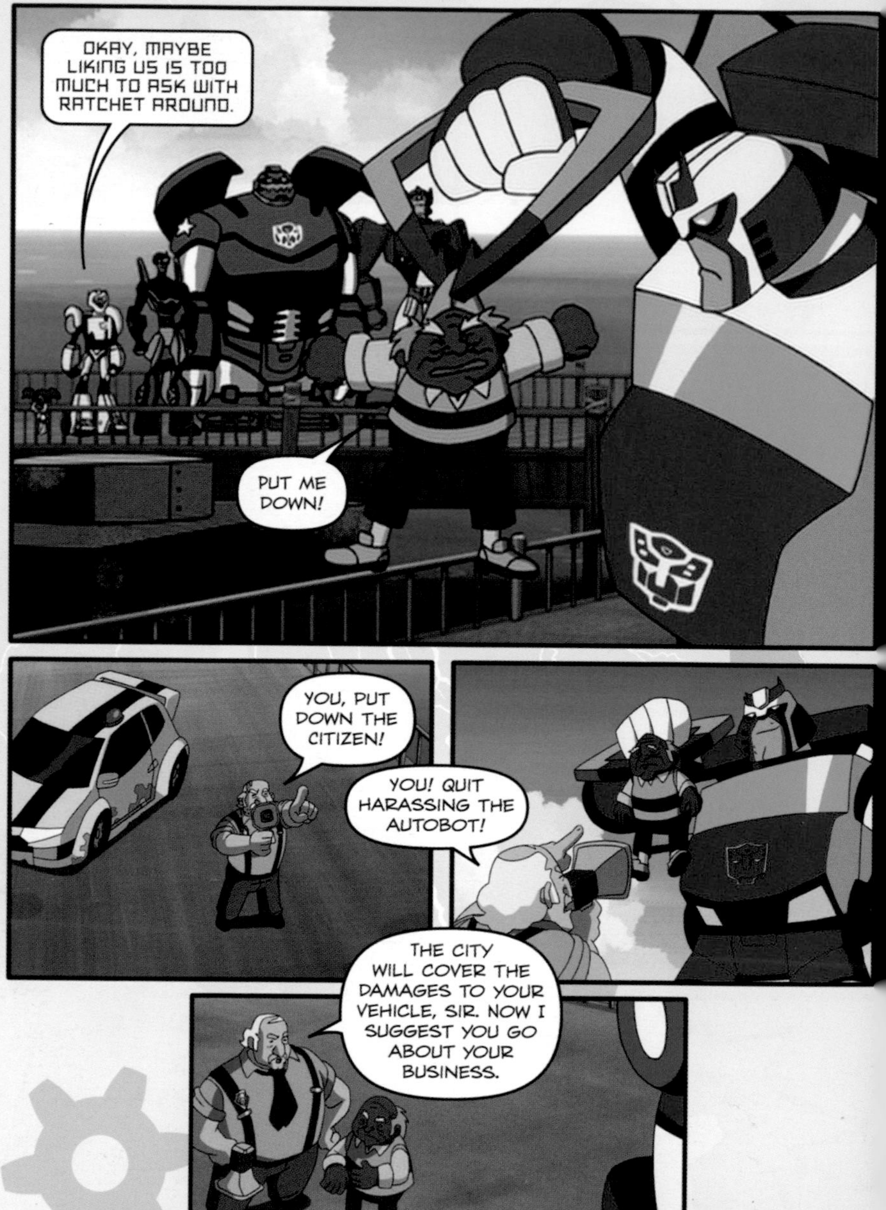
OKAY, MAYBE LIKING US IS TOO MUCH TO ASK WITH RATCHET AROUND.
PUT ME DOWN!
YOU, PUT DOWN THE CITIZEN!
YOU! QUIT HARASSING THE AUTOBOT!
THE CITY WILL COVER THE DAMAGES TO YOUR VEHICLE, SIR. NOW I SUGGEST YOU GO ABOUT YOUR BUSINESS.

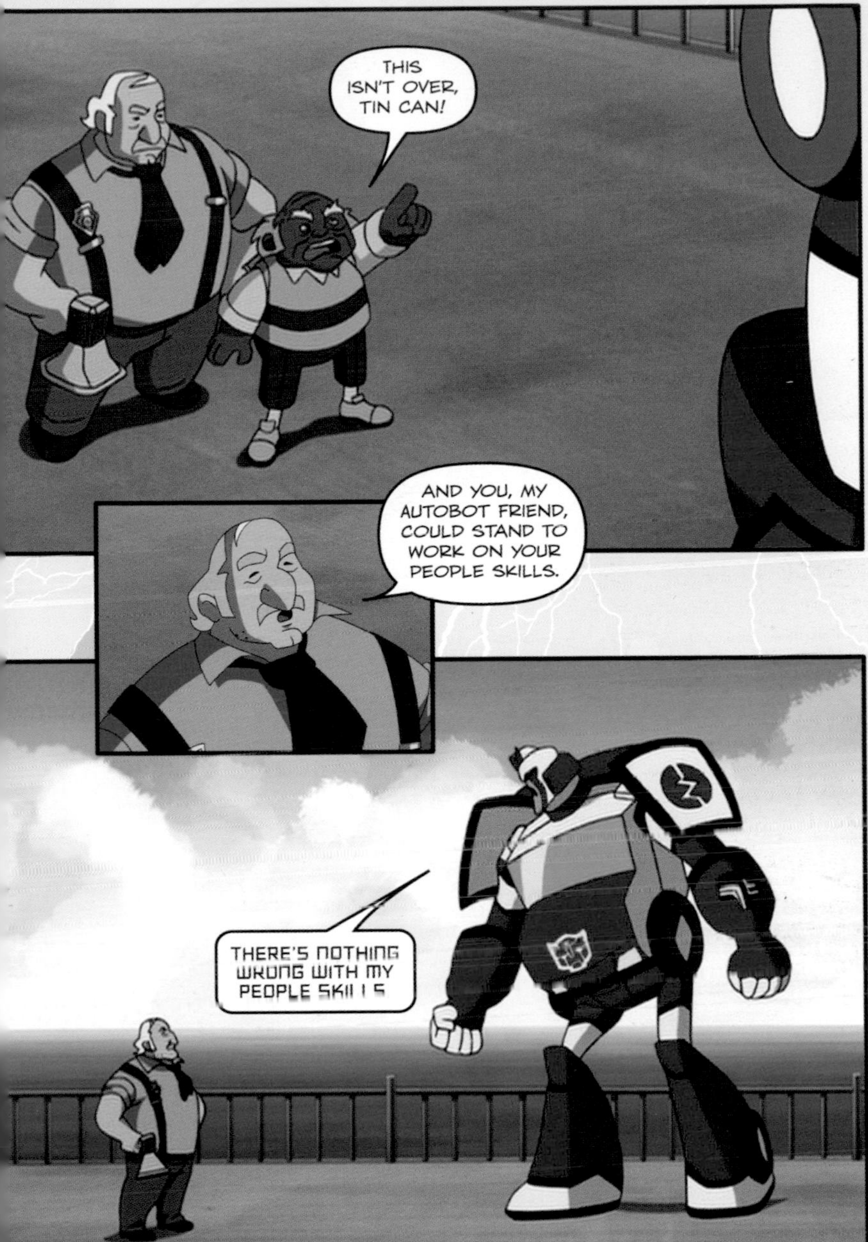
THIS ISN'T OVER, TIN CAN!
AND YOU, MY AUTOBOT FRIEND, COULD STAND TO WORK ON YOUR PEOPLE SKILLS.
THERE'S NOTHING WRONG WITH MY PEOPLE SKILLS

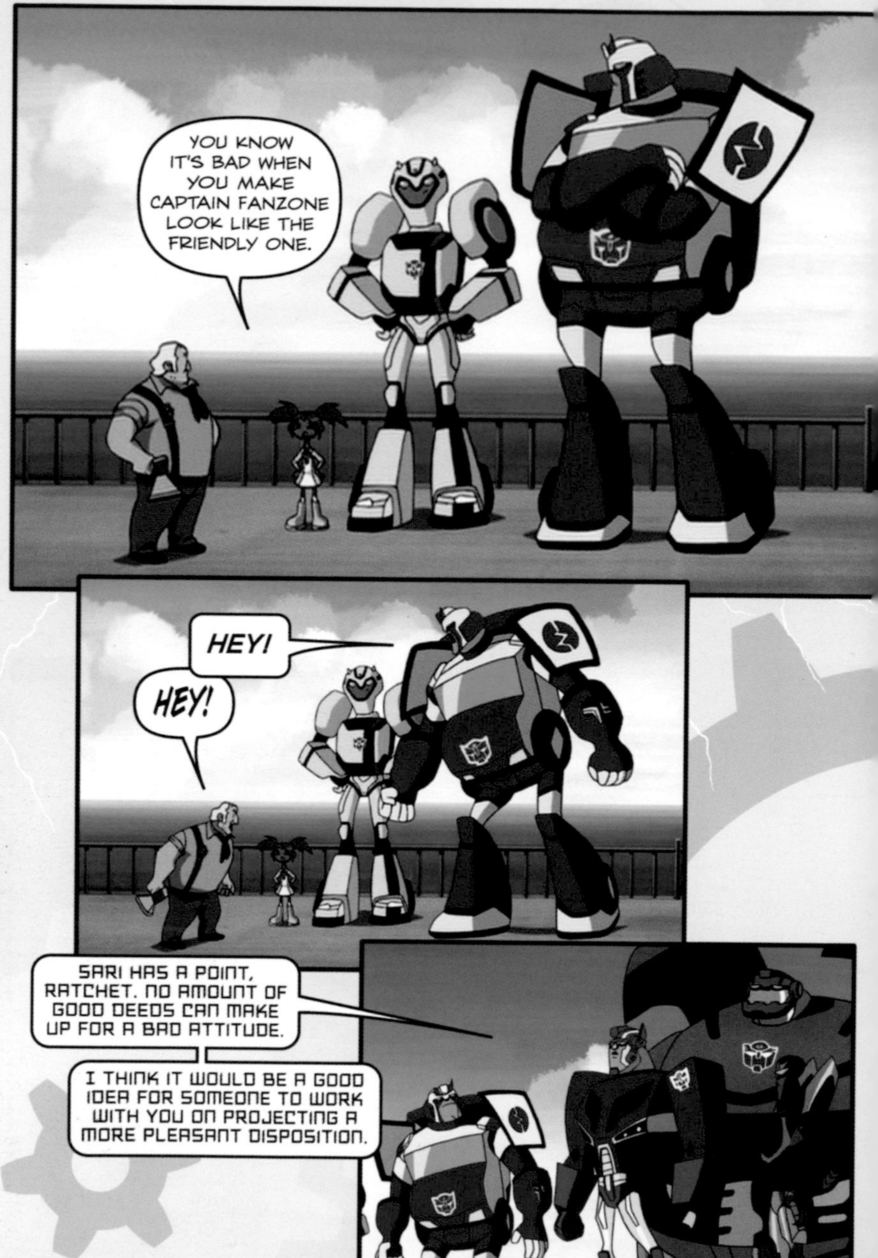
YOU KNOW IT'S BAD WHEN YOU MAKE CAPTAIN FANZONE LOOK LIKE THE FRIENDLY ONE.
HEY!
HEY!
SARI HAS A POINT, RATCHET. NO AMOUNT OF GOOD DEEDS CAN MAKE UP FOR A BAD ATTITUDE.
I THINK IT WOULD BE A GOOD IDEA FOR SOMEONE TO WORK WITH YOU ON PROJECTING A MORE PLEASANT DISPOSITION.

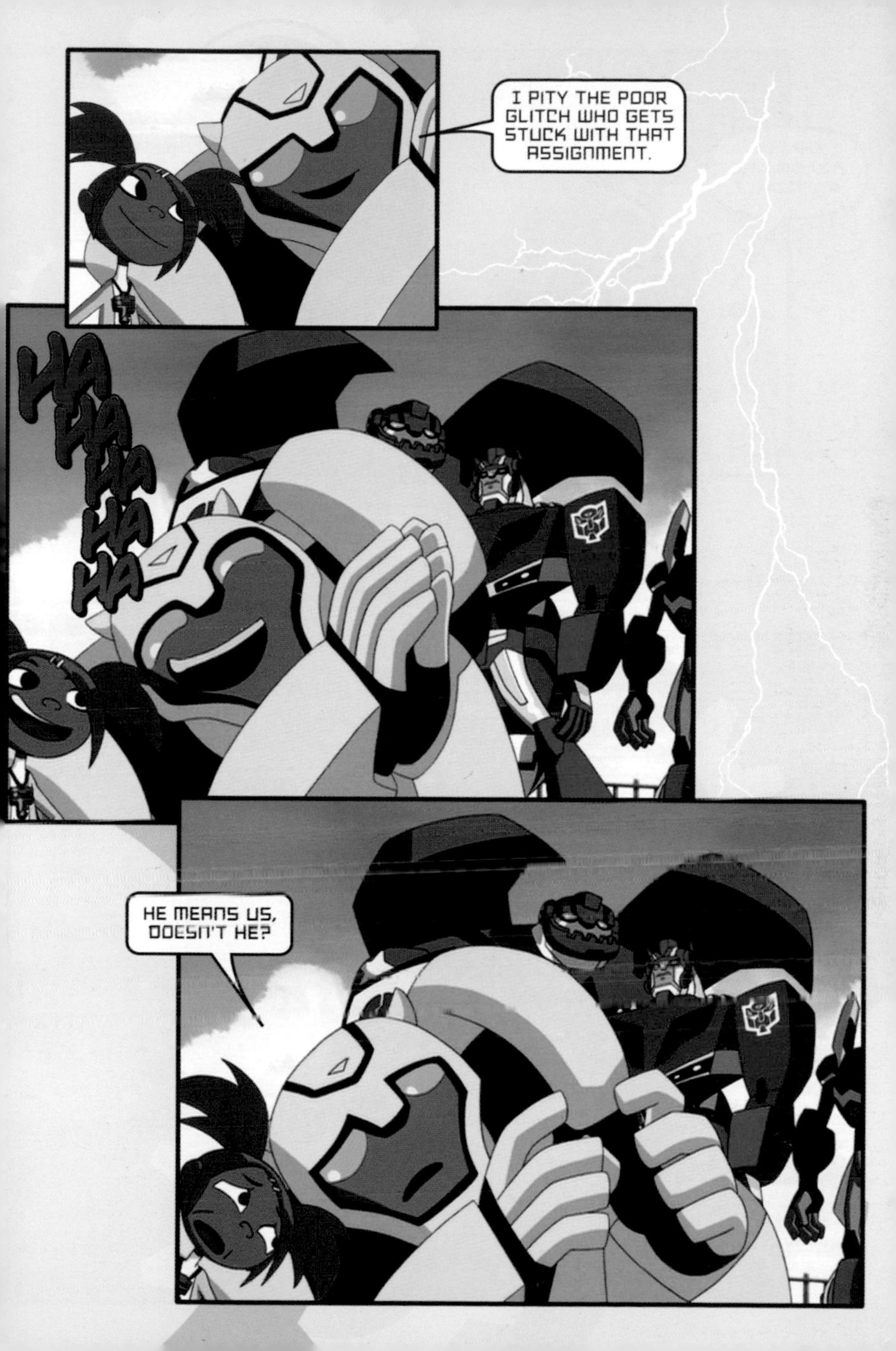
I PITY THE POOR GLITCH WHO GETS STUCK WITH THAT ASSIGNMENT.
HA HA HA HA HA HA
HE MEANS US, DOESN'T HE?

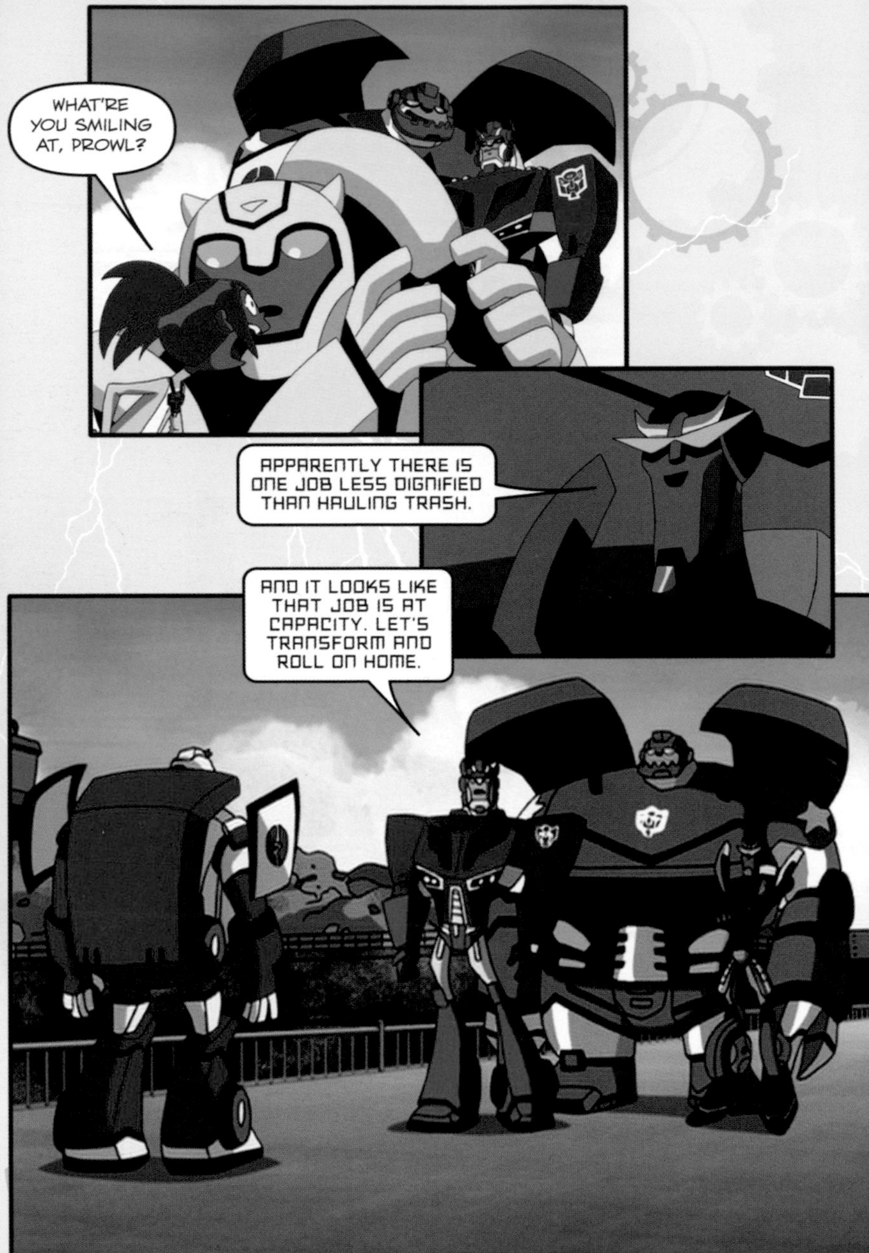
WHAT'RE YOU SMILING AT, PROWL?
APPARENTLY THERE IS ONE JOB LESS DIGNIFIED THAN HAULING TRASH.
AND IT LOOKS LIKE THAT JOB IS AT CAPACITY. LET'S TRANSFORM AND ROLL ON HOME.

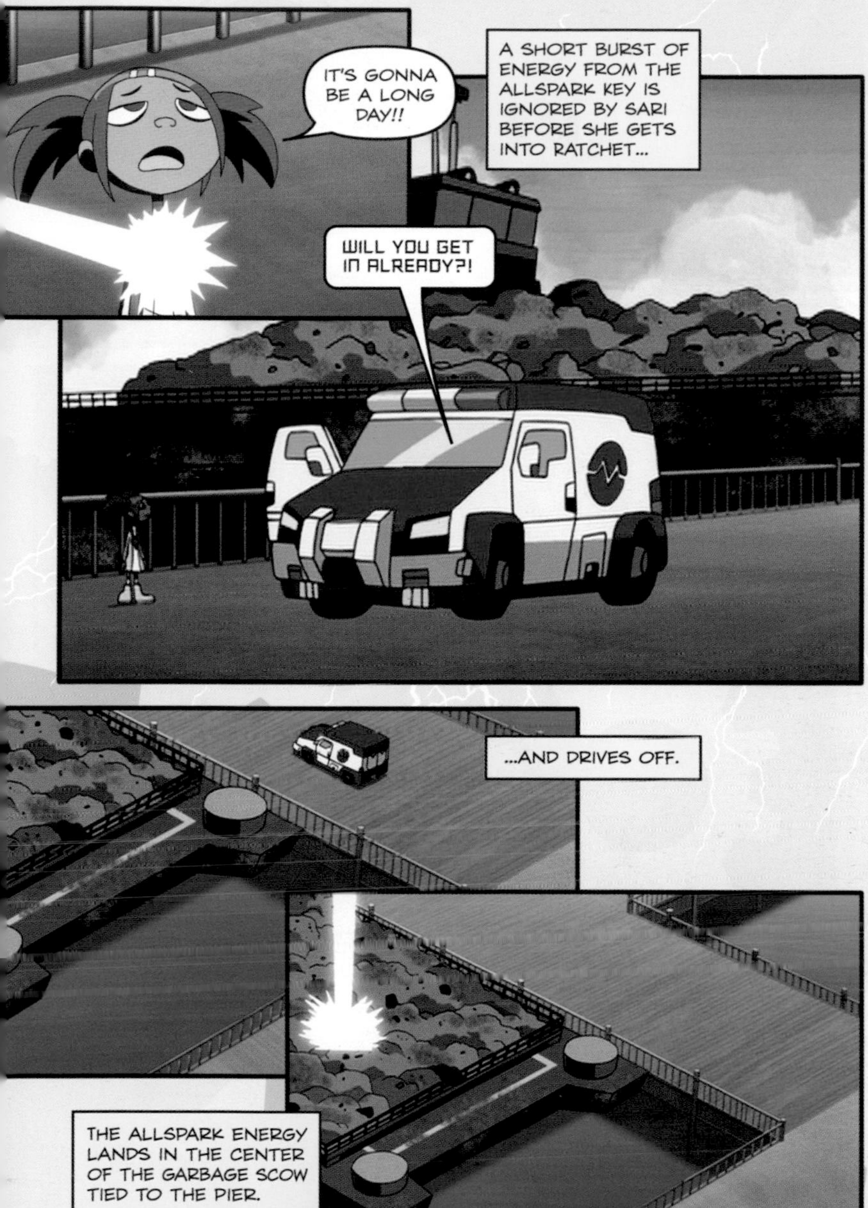
IT'S GONNA BE A LONG DAY!!
A SHORT BURST OF ENERGY FROM THE ALLSPARK KEY IS IGNORED BY SARI BEFORE SHE GETS INTO RATCHET...
WILL YOU GET IN ALREADY?!
...AND DRIVES OFF.
THE ALLSPARK ENERGY LANDS IN THE CENTER OF THE GARBAGE SCOW TIED TO THE PIER.

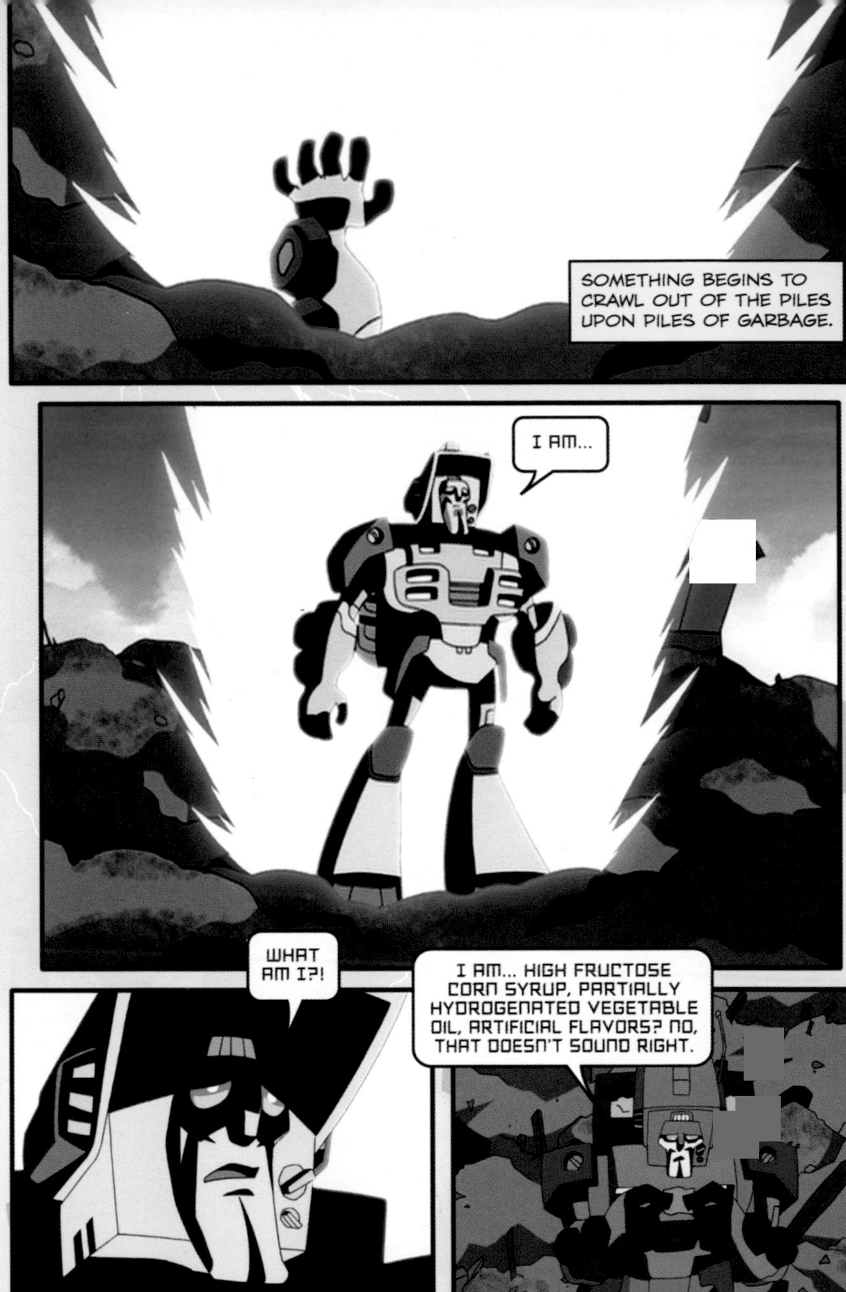
SOMETHING BEGINS TO CRAWL OUT OF THE PILES UPON PILES OF GARBAGE.
I AM...
WHAT AM I?!
I AM... HIGH FRUCTOSE CORN SYRUP, PARTIALLY HYDROGENATED VEGETABLE OIL, ARTIFICIAL FLAVORS? NO, THAT DOESN'T SOUND RIGHT.

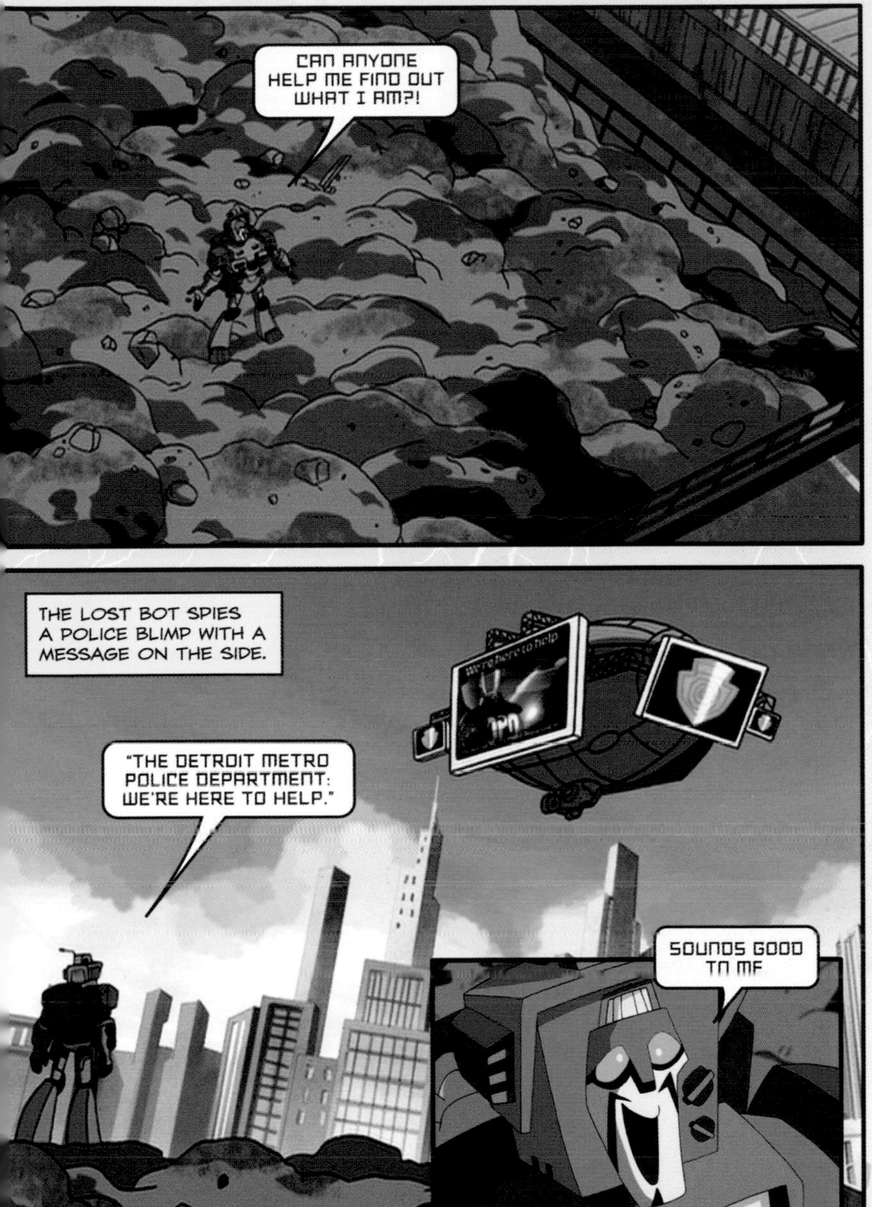
CAN ANYONE HELP ME FIND OUT WHAT I AM?!
THE LOST BOT SPIES A POLICE BLIMP WITH A MESSAGE ON THE SIDE.
"THE DETROIT METRO POLICE DEPARTMENT: WE'RE HERE TO HELP."
SOUNDS GOOD TO ME

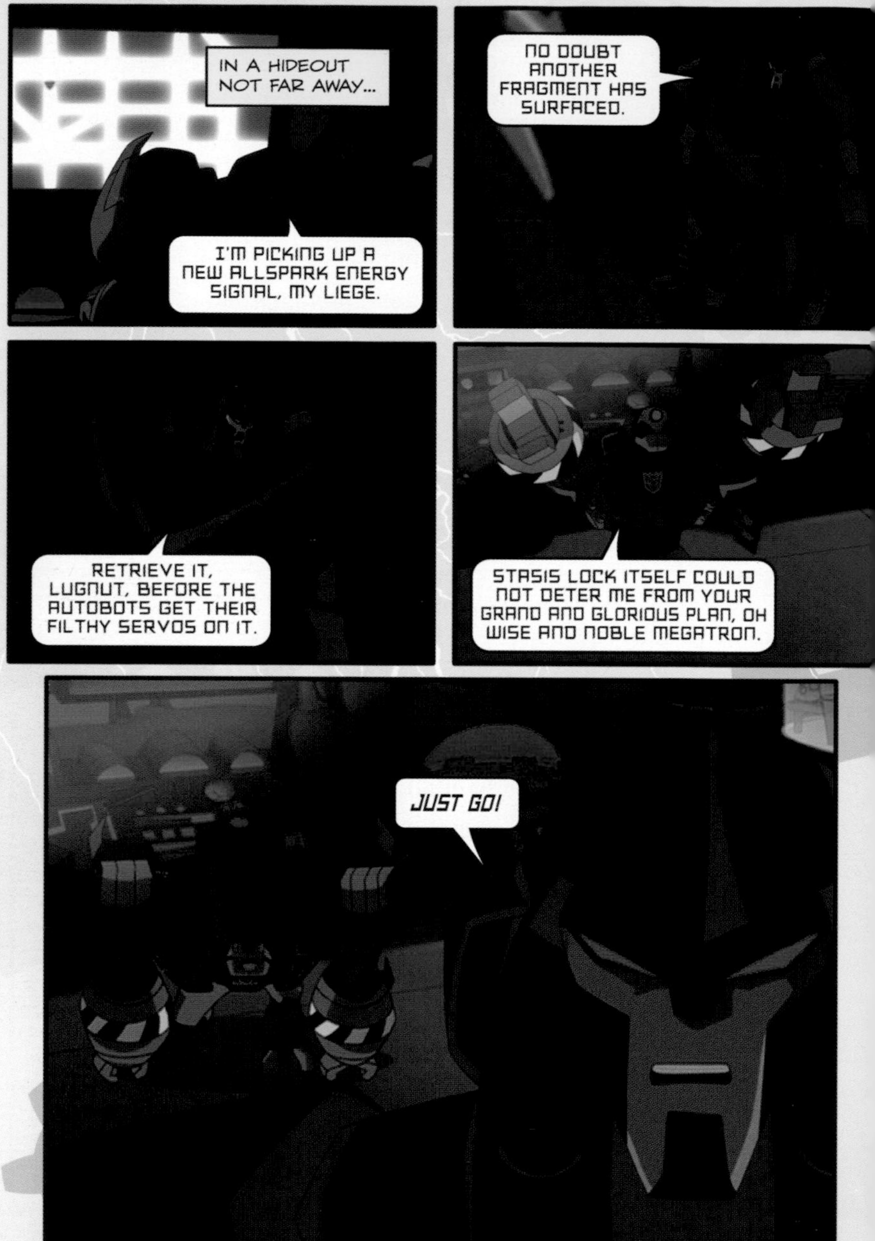
IN A HIDEOUT NOT FAR AWAY...
I'M PICKING UP A NEW ALLSPARK ENERGY SIGNAL, MY LIEGE.
NO DOUBT ANOTHER FRAGMENT HAS SURFACED.
RETRIEVE IT, LUGNUT, BEFORE THE AUTOBOTS GET THEIR FILTHY SERVOS ON IT.
STASIS LOCK ITSELF COULD NOT DETER ME FROM YOUR GRAND AND GLORIOUS PLAN, OH WISE AND NOBLE MEGATRON.
JUST GO!

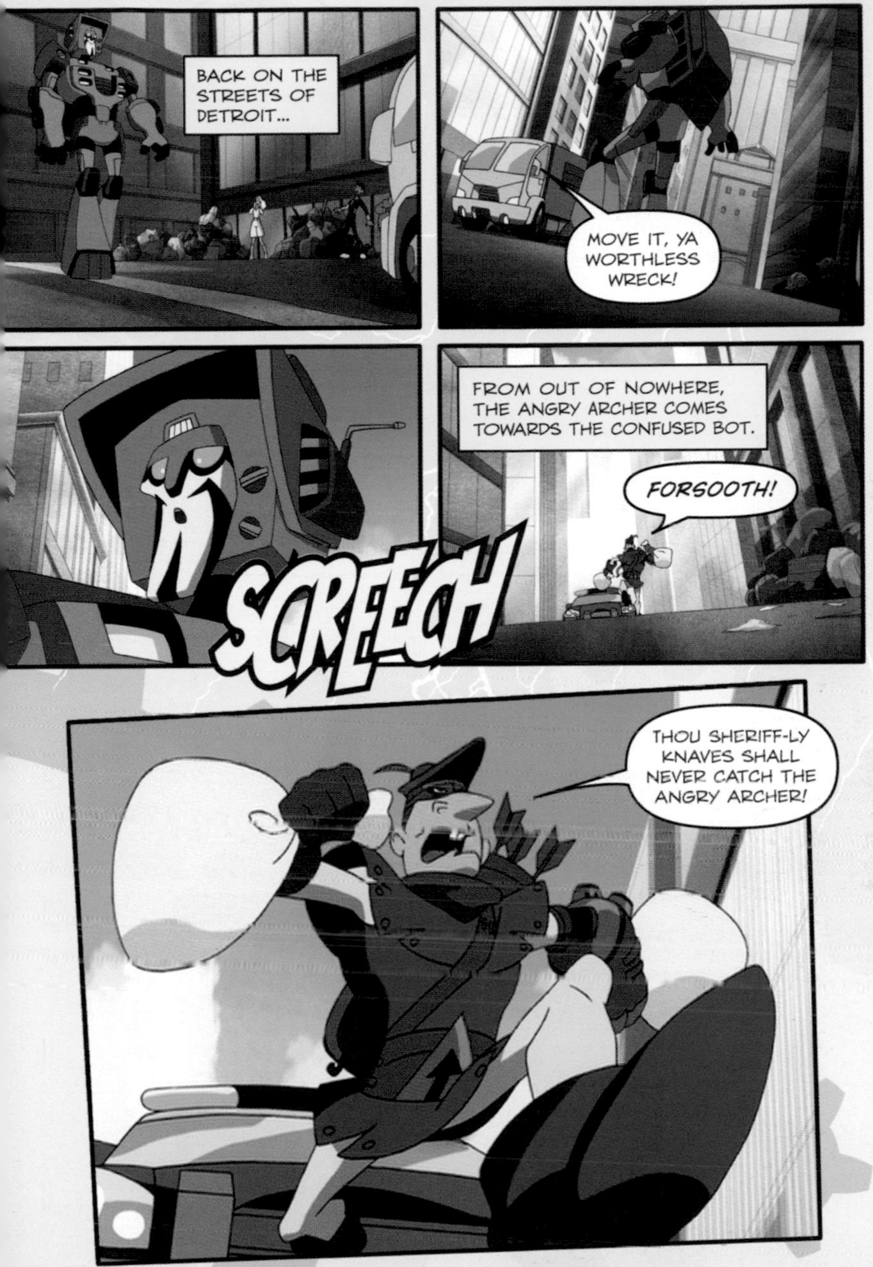
BACK ON THE STREETS OF DETROIT...
MOVE IT, YA WORTHLESS WRECK!
FROM OUT OF NOWHERE, THE ANGRY ARCHER COMES TOWARDS THE CONFUSED BOT.
FORSOOTH!
SCREECH
THOU SHERIFF-LY KNAVES SHALL NEVER CATCH THE ANGRY ARCHER!

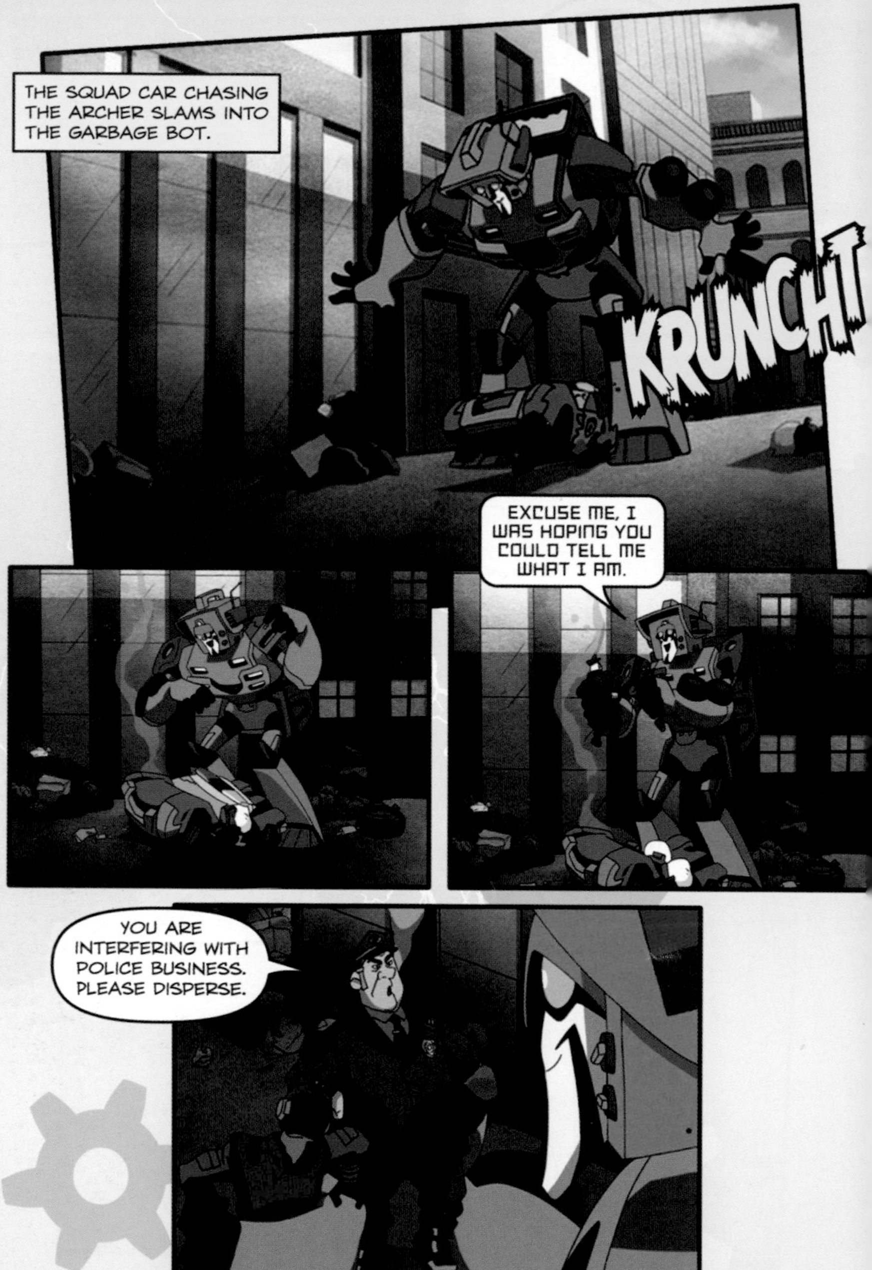
THE SQUAD CAR CHASING THE ARCHER SLAMS INTO THE GARBAGE BOT.
KRUNCH
EXCUSE ME, I WAS HOPING YOU COULD TELL ME WHAT I AM.
YOU ARE INTERFERING WITH POLICE BUSINESS. PLEASE DISPERSE.

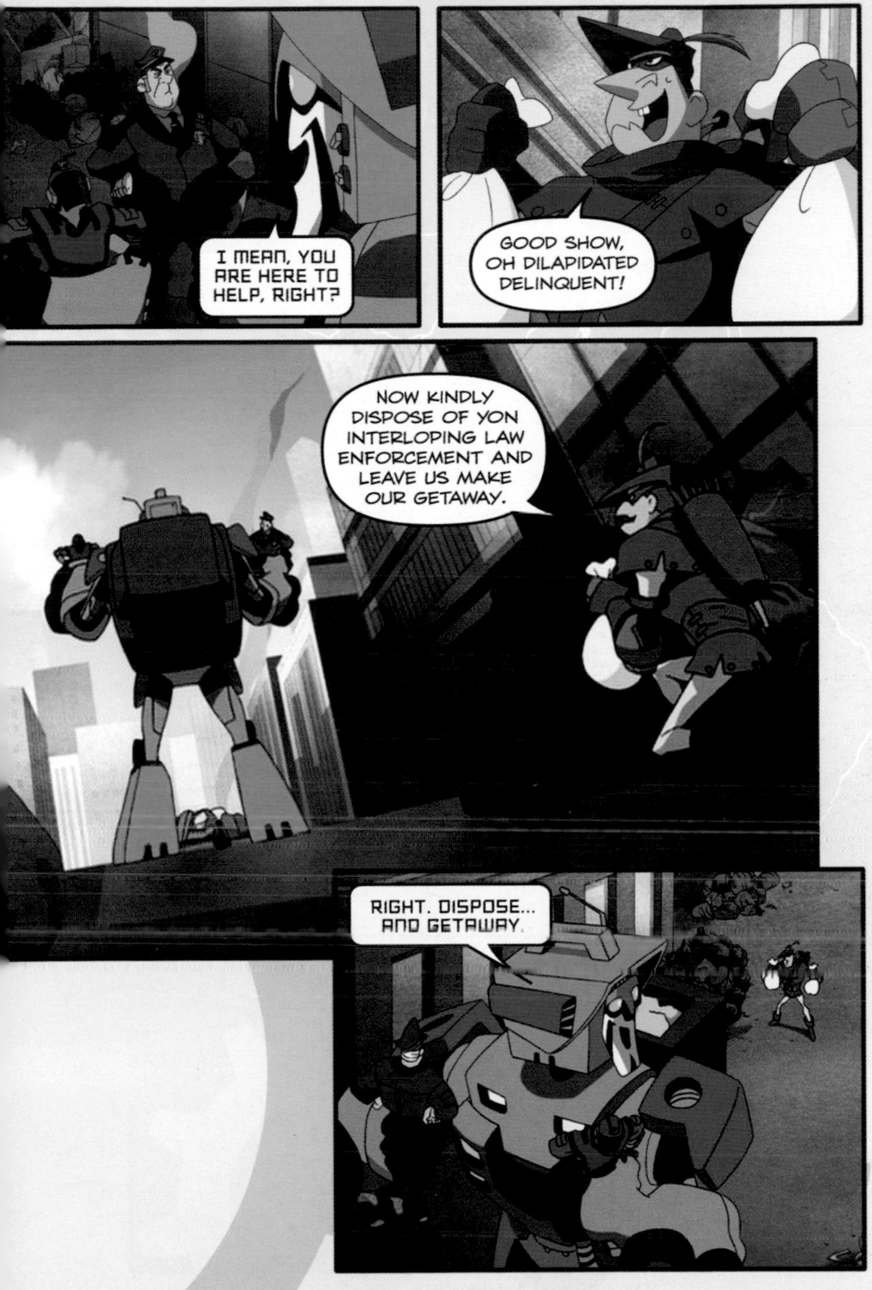
I MEAN, YOU ARE HERE TO HELP, RIGHT?
GOOD SHOW, OH DILAPIDATED DELINQUENT!
NOW KINDLY DISPOSE OF YON INTERLOPING LAW ENFORCEMENT AND LEAVE US MAKE OUR GETAWAY.
RIGHT. DISPOSE... ...AND GETAWAY.

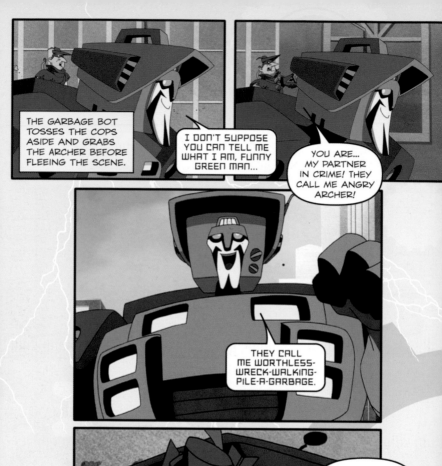

THE GARBAGE BOT TOSSES THE COPS ASIDE AND GRABS THE ARCHER BEFORE FLEEING THE SCENE.

I DON'T SUPPOSE YOU CAN TELL ME WHAT I AM, FUNNY GREEN MAN...

YOU ARE... MY PARTNER IN CRIME! THEY CALL ME ANGRY ARCHER!

THEY CALL ME WORTHLESS-WRECK-WALKING-PILE-A-GARBAGE.

HMMM... BIT OF A MOUTHFUL. PERHAPS WE SHOULD JUST CALL YOU WRECK-GAR FOR SHORT.

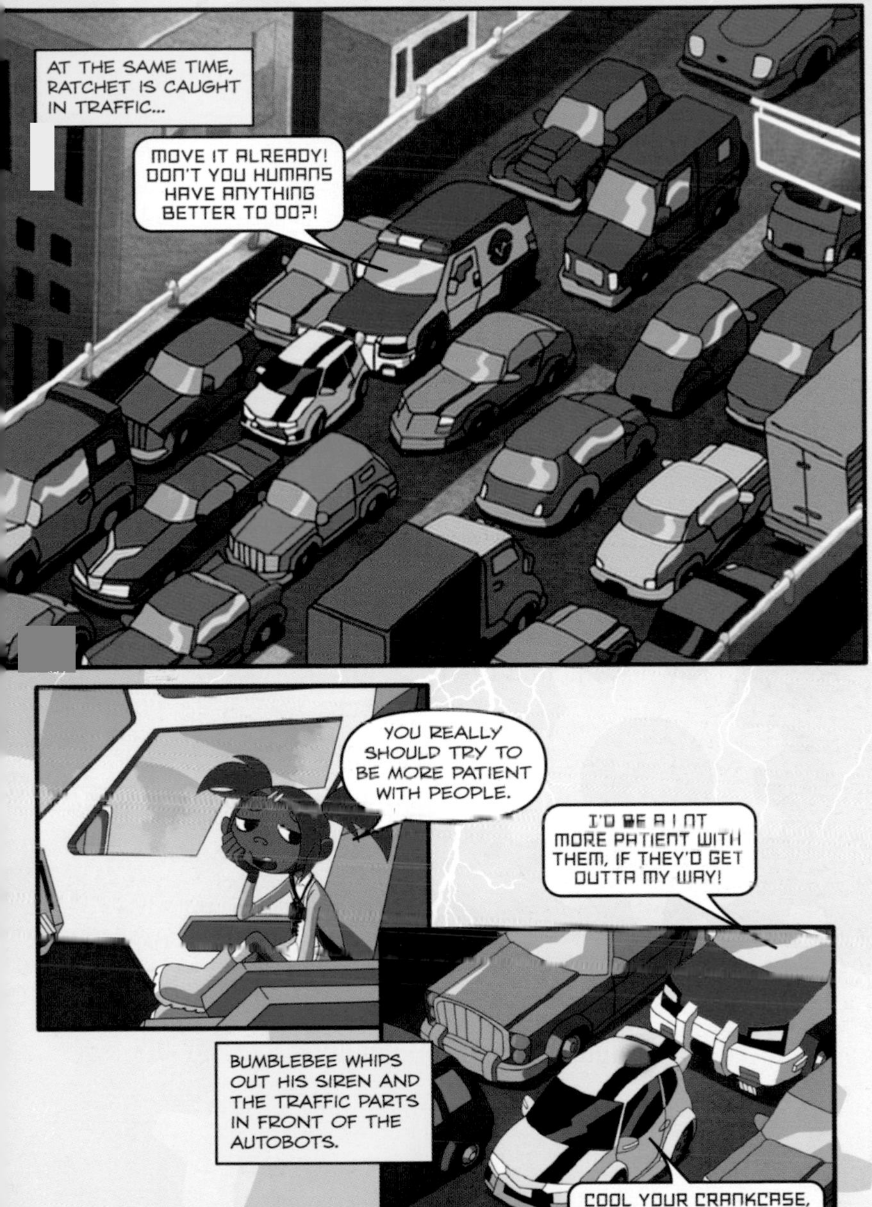
AT THE SAME TIME, RATCHET IS CAUGHT IN TRAFFIC...
MOVE IT ALREADY! DON'T YOU HUMANS HAVE ANYTHING BETTER TO DO?!
YOU REALLY SHOULD TRY TO BE MORE PATIENT WITH PEOPLE.
I'D BE A LOT MORE PATIENT WITH THEM, IF THEY'D GET OUTTA MY WAY!
BUMBLEBEE WHIPS OUT HIS SIREN AND THE TRAFFIC PARTS IN FRONT OF THE AUTOBOTS.
COOL YOUR CRANKCASE, RATCHET. THAT'S WHAT THESE THINGS ARE FOR.

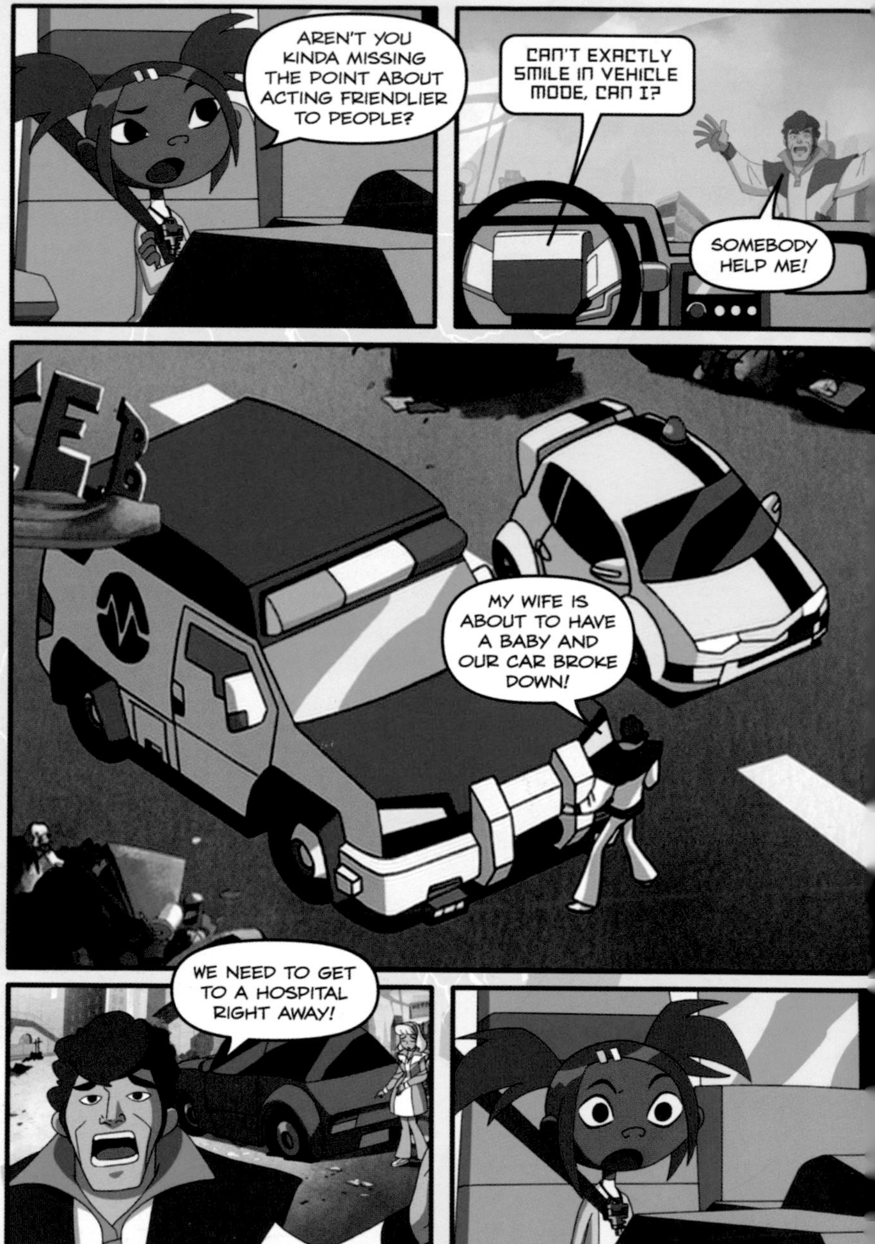

AREN'T YOU KINDA MISSING THE POINT ABOUT ACTING FRIENDLIER TO PEOPLE?
CAN'T EXACTLY SMILE IN VEHICLE MODE, CAN I?
SOMEBODY HELP ME!
MY WIFE IS ABOUT TO HAVE A BABY AND OUR CAR BROKE DOWN!
WE NEED TO GET TO A HOSPITAL RIGHT AWAY!

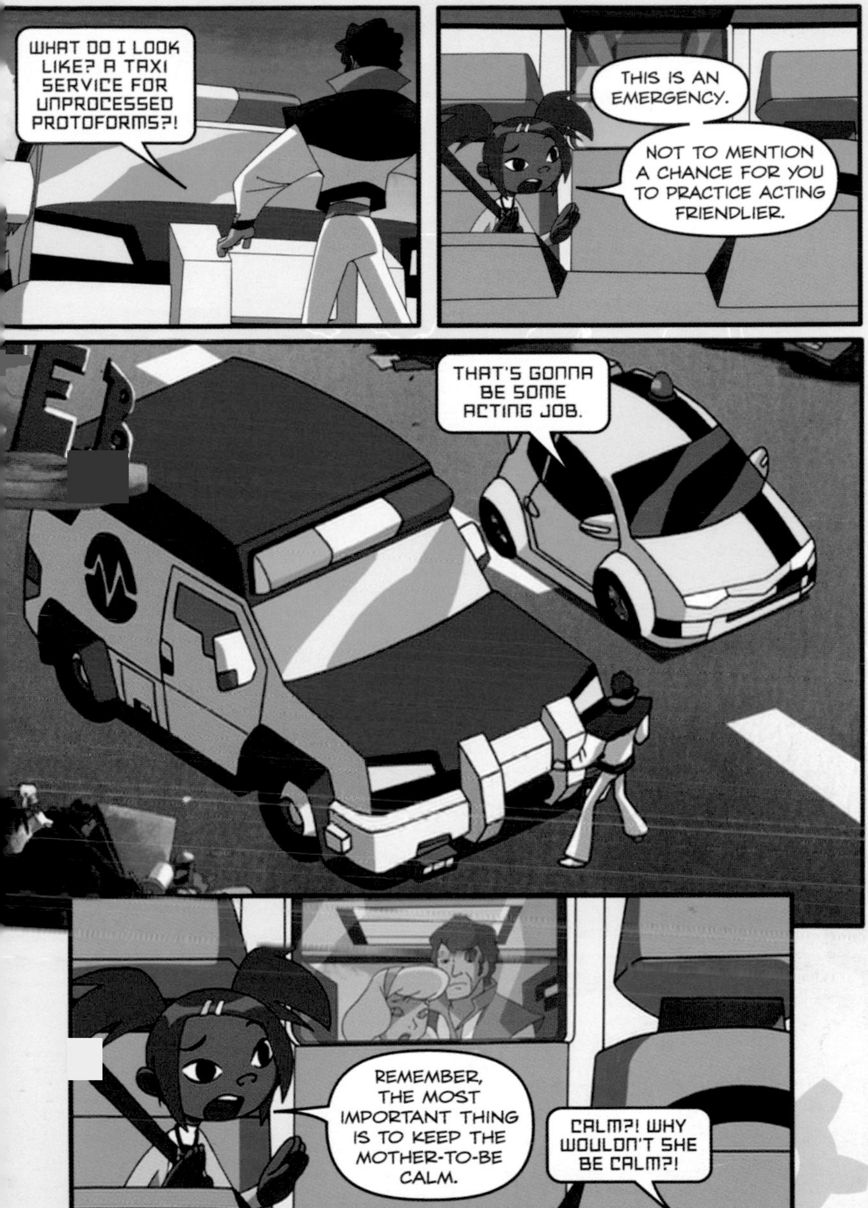
WHAT DO I LOOK LIKE? A TAXI SERVICE FOR UNPROCESSED PROTOFORMS?!
THIS IS AN EMERGENCY.
NOT TO MENTION A CHANCE FOR YOU TO PRACTICE ACTING FRIENDLIER.
THAT'S GONNA BE SOME ACTING JOB.
REMEMBER, THE MOST IMPORTANT THING IS TO KEEP THE MOTHER-TO-BE CALM.
CALM?! WHY WOULDN'T SHE BE CALM?!

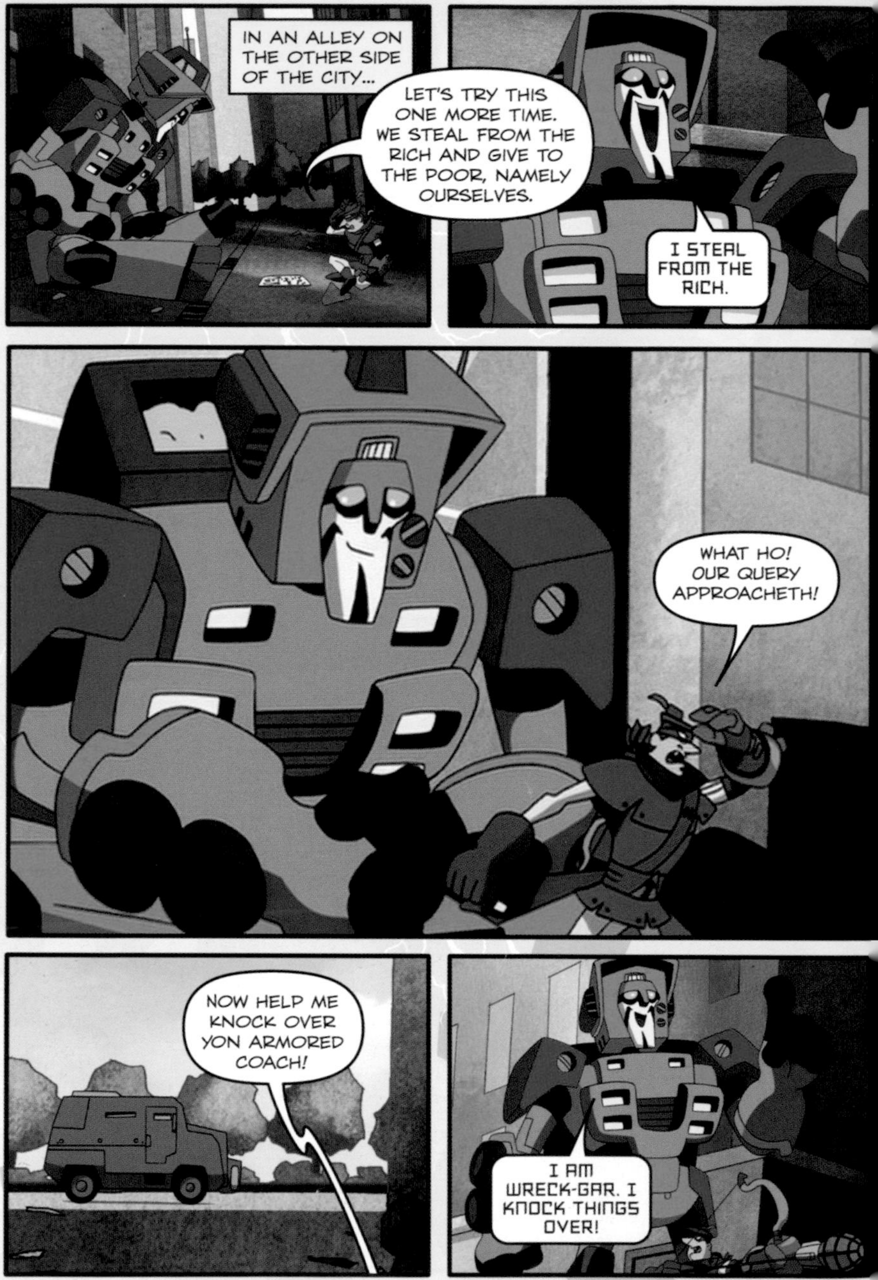
IN AN ALLEY ON THE OTHER SIDE OF THE CITY...
LET'S TRY THIS ONE MORE TIME. WE STEAL FROM THE RICH AND GIVE TO THE POOR, NAMELY OURSELVES.
I STEAL FROM THE RICH.
WHAT HO! OUR QUERY APPROACHETH!
NOW HELP ME KNOCK OVER YON ARMORED COACH!
I AM WRECK-GAR. I KNOCK THINGS OVER!

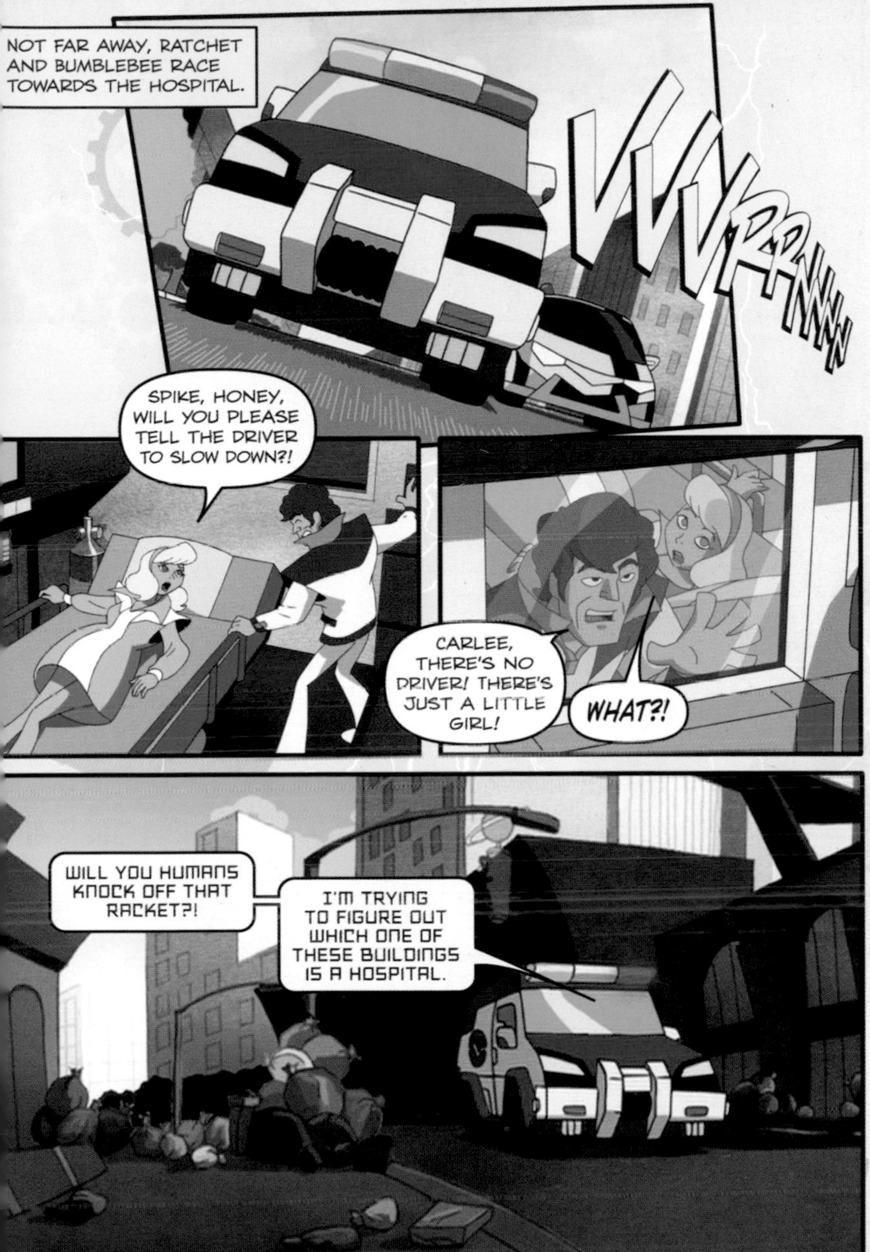
NOT FAR AWAY, RATCHET AND BUMBLEBEE RACE TOWARDS THE HOSPITAL.
VVVRRNNN
SPIKE, HONEY, WILL YOU PLEASE TELL THE DRIVER TO SLOW DOWN?!
CARLEE, THERE'S NO DRIVER! THERE'S JUST A LITTLE GIRL!
WHAT?!
WILL YOU HUMANS KNOCK OFF THAT RACKET?!
I'M TRYING TO FIGURE OUT WHICH ONE OF THESE BUILDINGS IS A HOSPITAL.

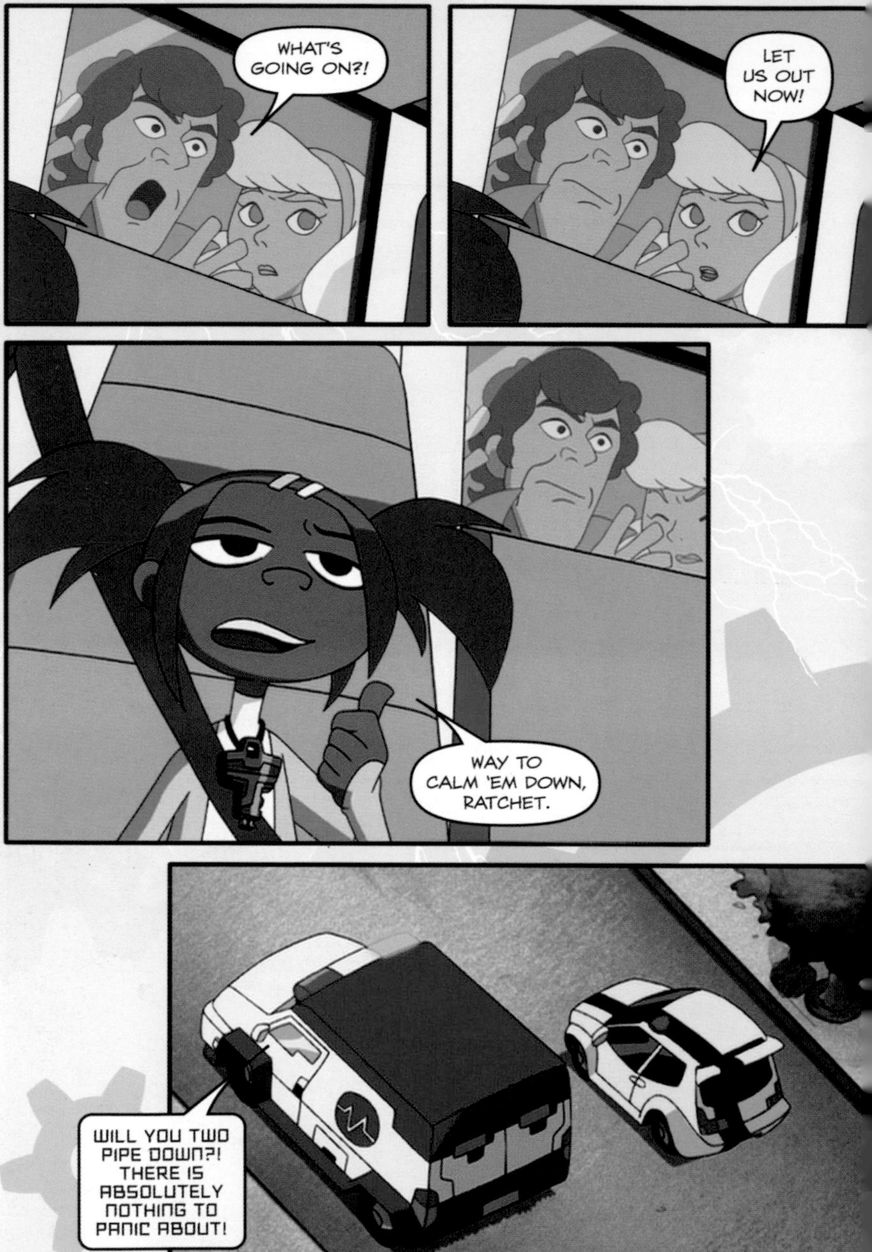

WHAT'S GOING ON?!
LET US OUT NOW!
WAY TO CALM 'EM DOWN, RATCHET.
WILL YOU TWO PIPE DOWN?! THERE IS ABSOLUTELY NOTHING TO PANIC ABOUT!

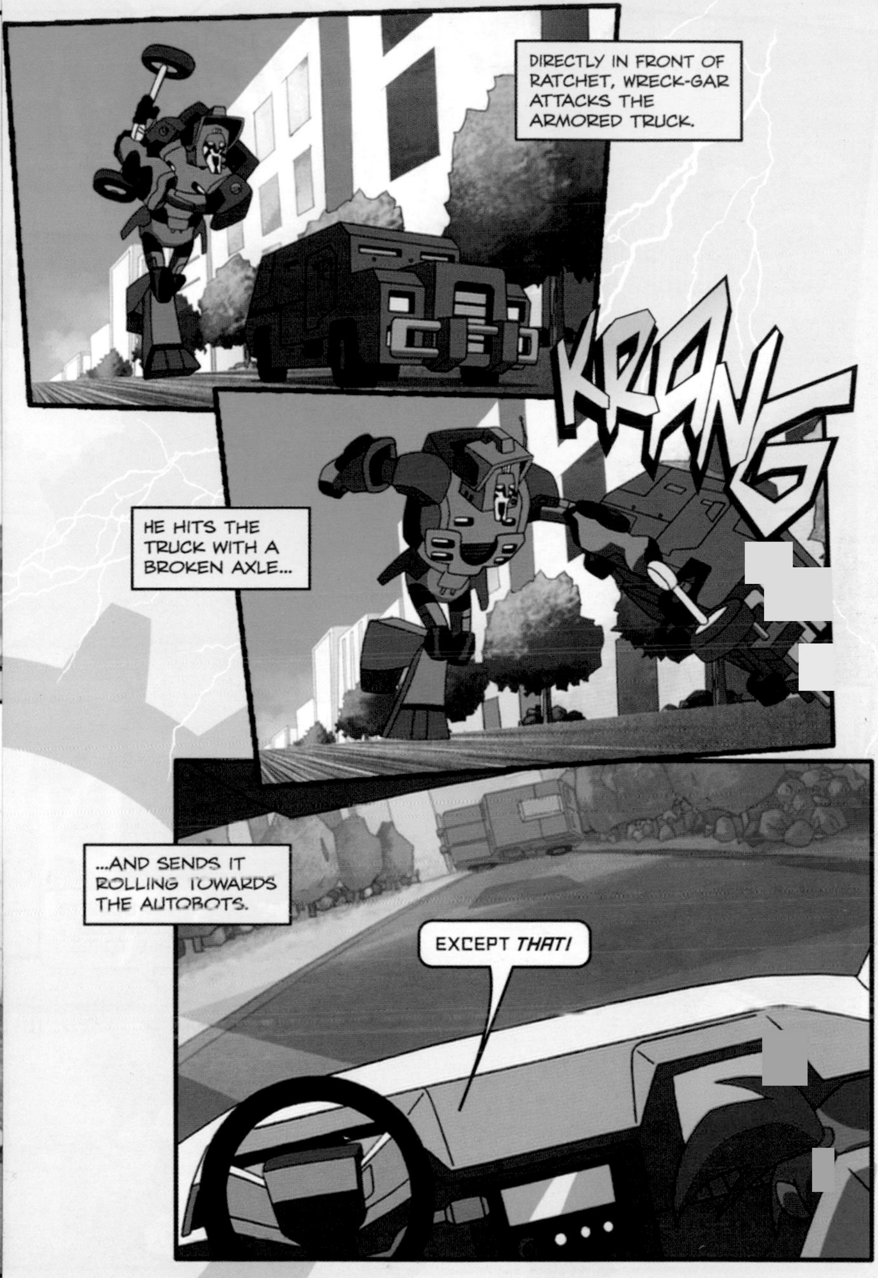
DIRECTLY IN FRONT OF RATCHET, WRECK-GAR ATTACKS THE ARMORED TRUCK.
KRANG
HE HITS THE TRUCK WITH A BROKEN AXLE...
...AND SENDS IT ROLLING TOWARDS THE AUTOBOTS.
EXCEPT *THAT!*

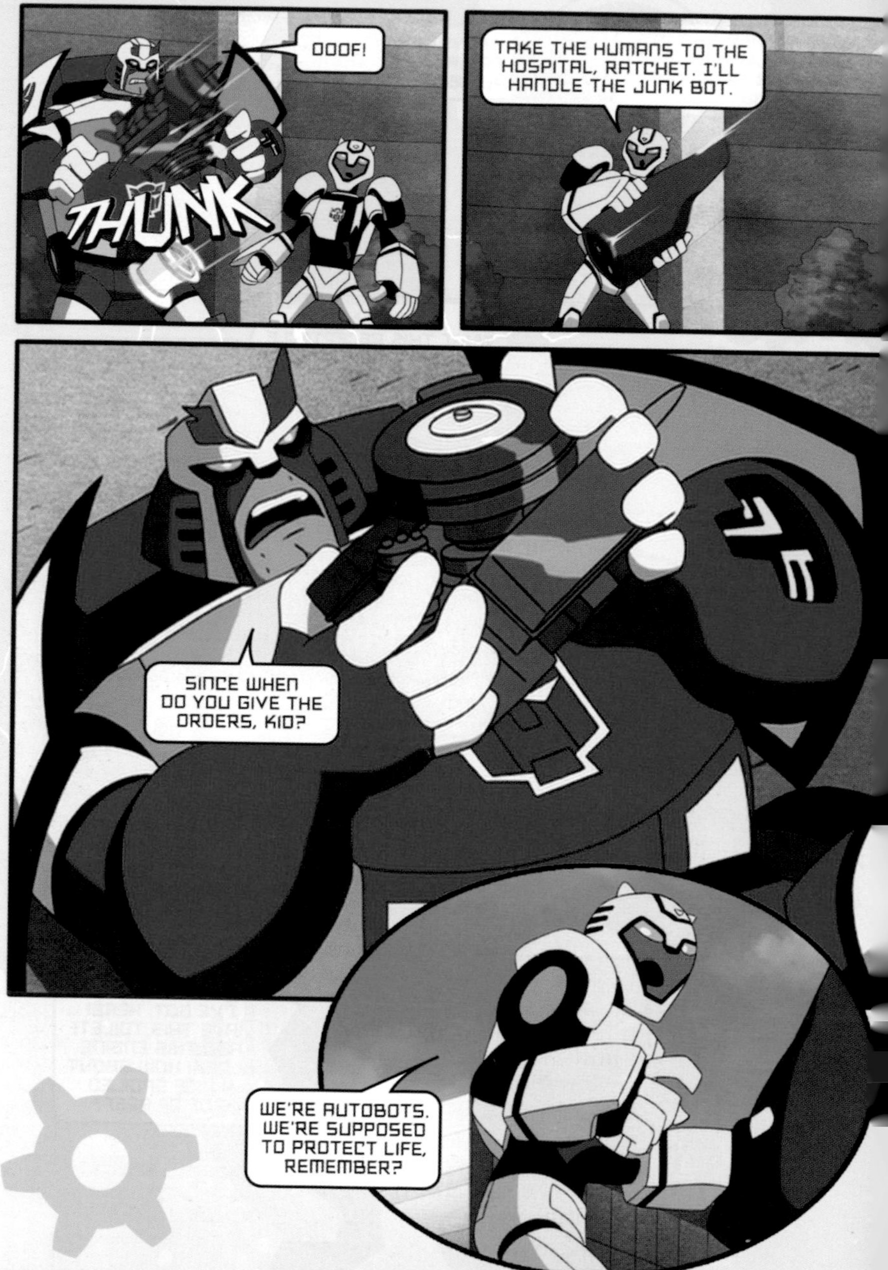
OOOF!
THUNK
TAKE THE HUMANS TO THE HOSPITAL, RATCHET. I'LL HANDLE THE JUNK BOT.
SINCE WHEN DO YOU GIVE THE ORDERS, KID?
WE'RE AUTOBOTS. WE'RE SUPPOSED TO PROTECT LIFE, REMEMBER?

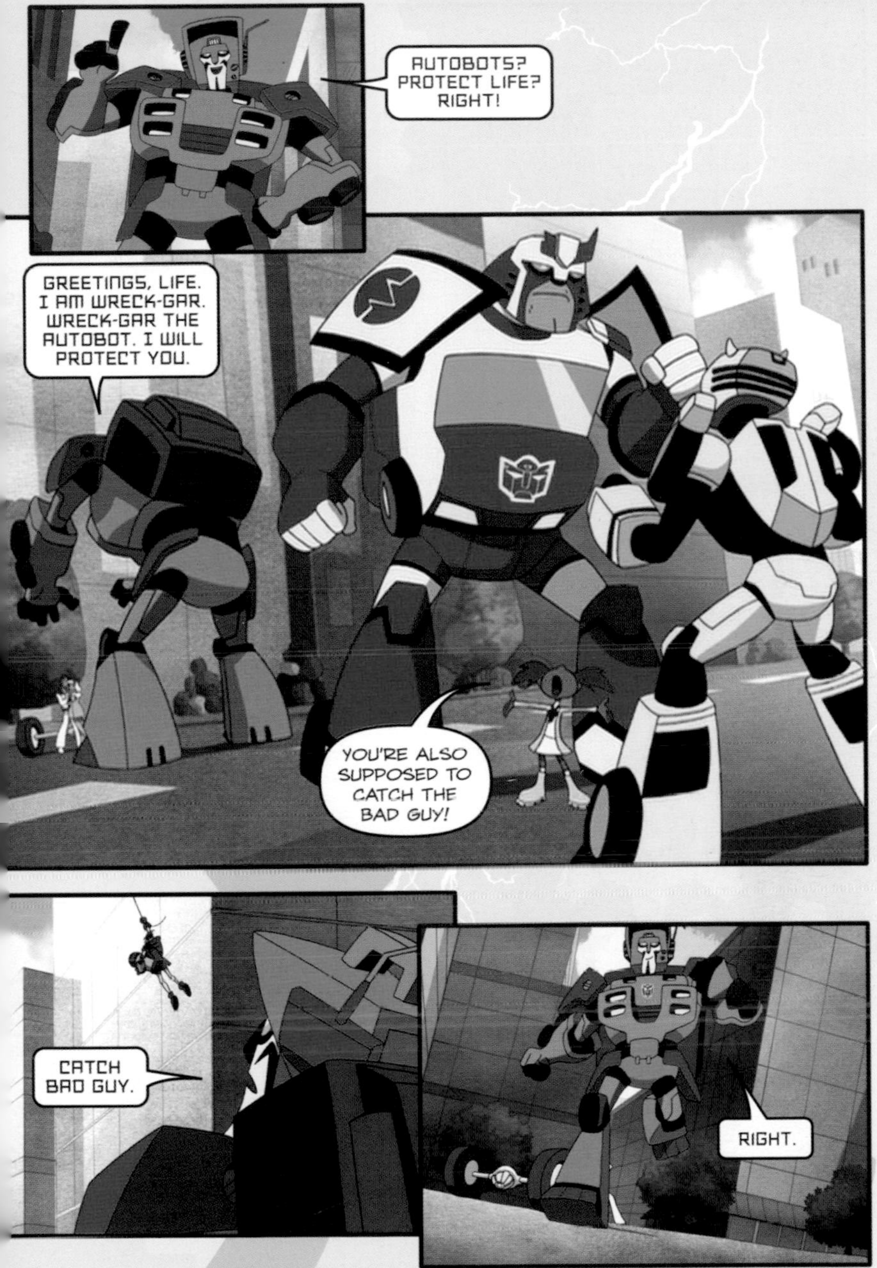
AUTOBOTS? PROTECT LIFE? RIGHT!
GREETINGS, LIFE. I AM WRECK-GAR. WRECK-GAR THE AUTOBOT. I WILL PROTECT YOU.
YOU'RE ALSO SUPPOSED TO CATCH THE BAD GUY!
CATCH BAD GUY.
RIGHT.

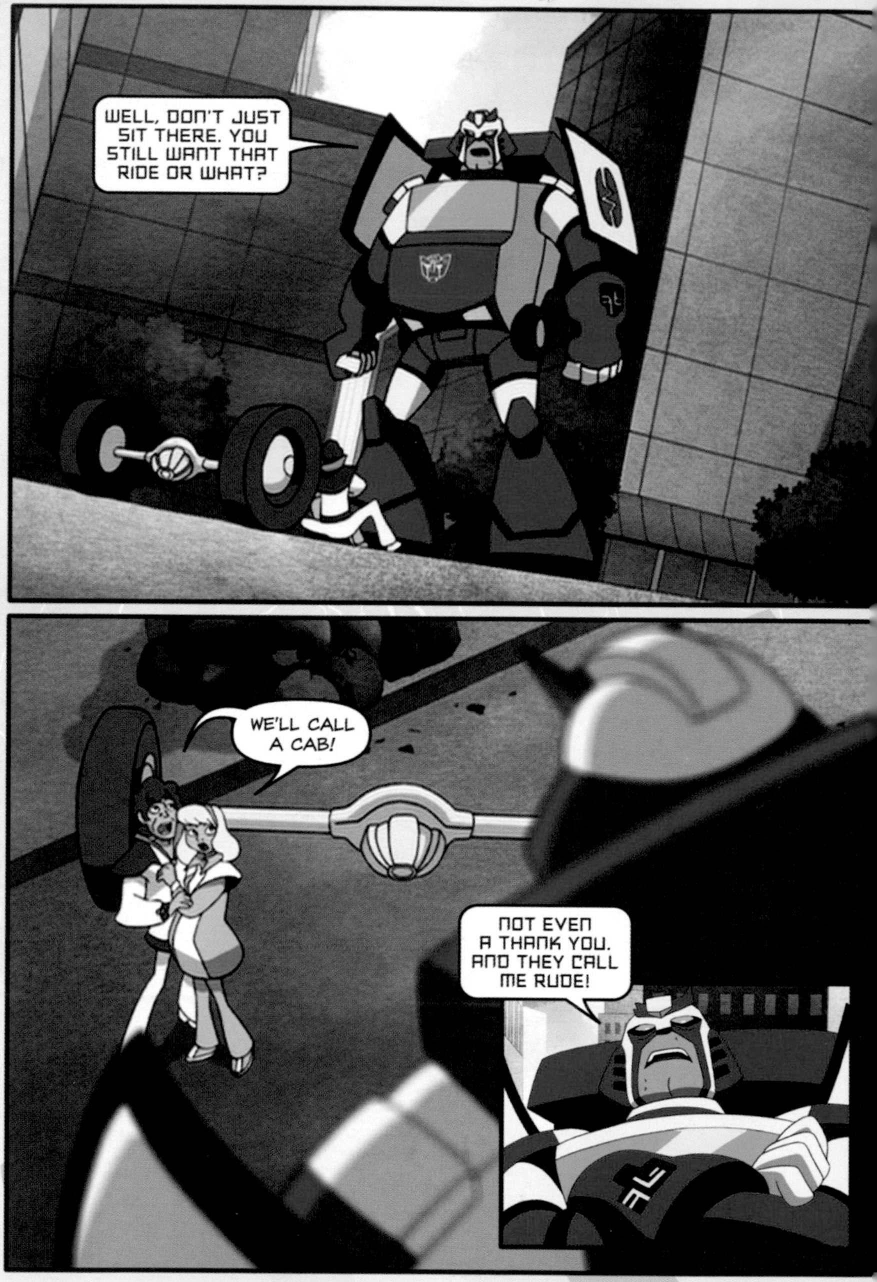
WELL, DON'T JUST SIT THERE. YOU STILL WANT THAT RIDE OR WHAT?
WE'LL CALL A CAB!
NOT EVEN A THANK YOU. AND THEY CALL ME RUDE!

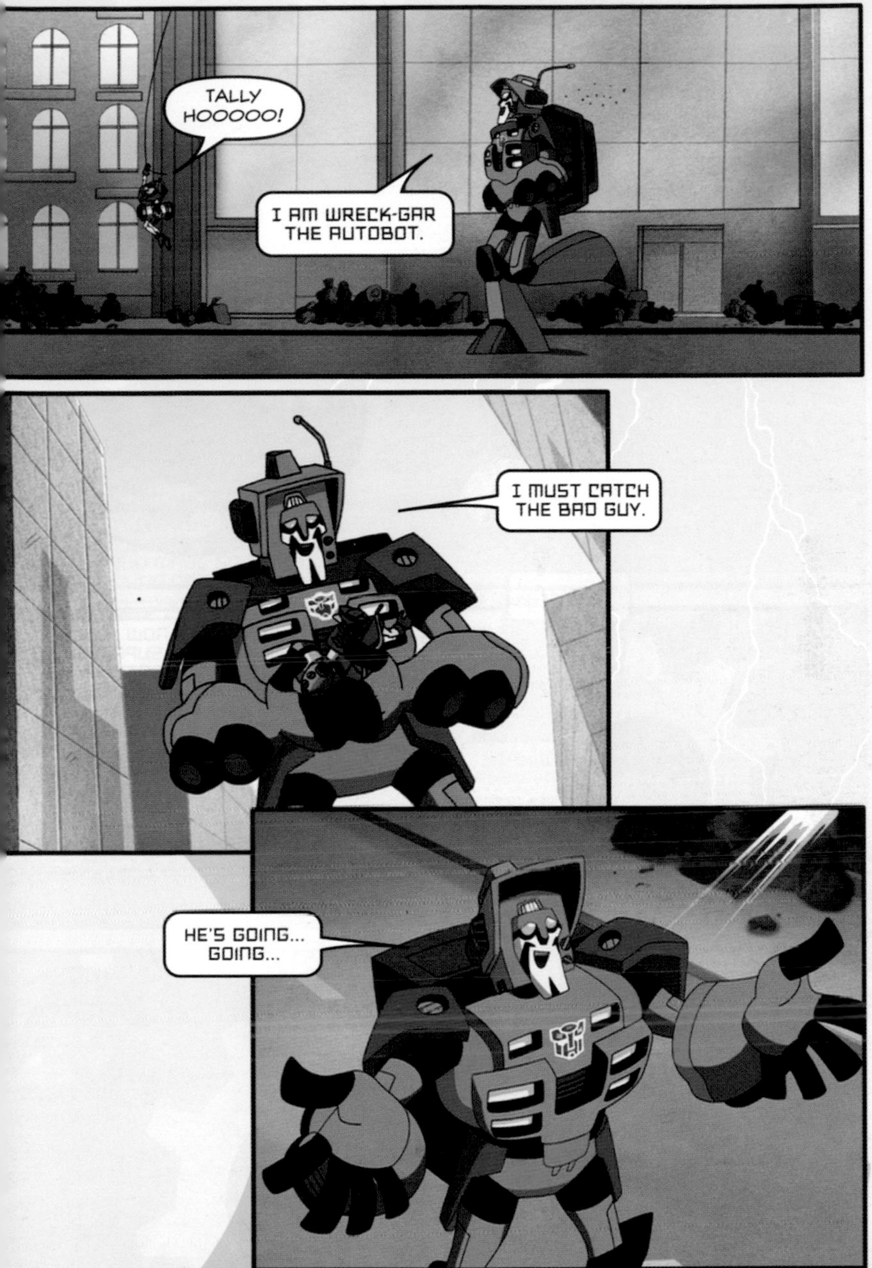
TALLY HOOOOO!
I AM WRECK-GAR THE AUTOBOT.
I MUST CATCH THE BAD GUY.
HE'S GOING... GOING...

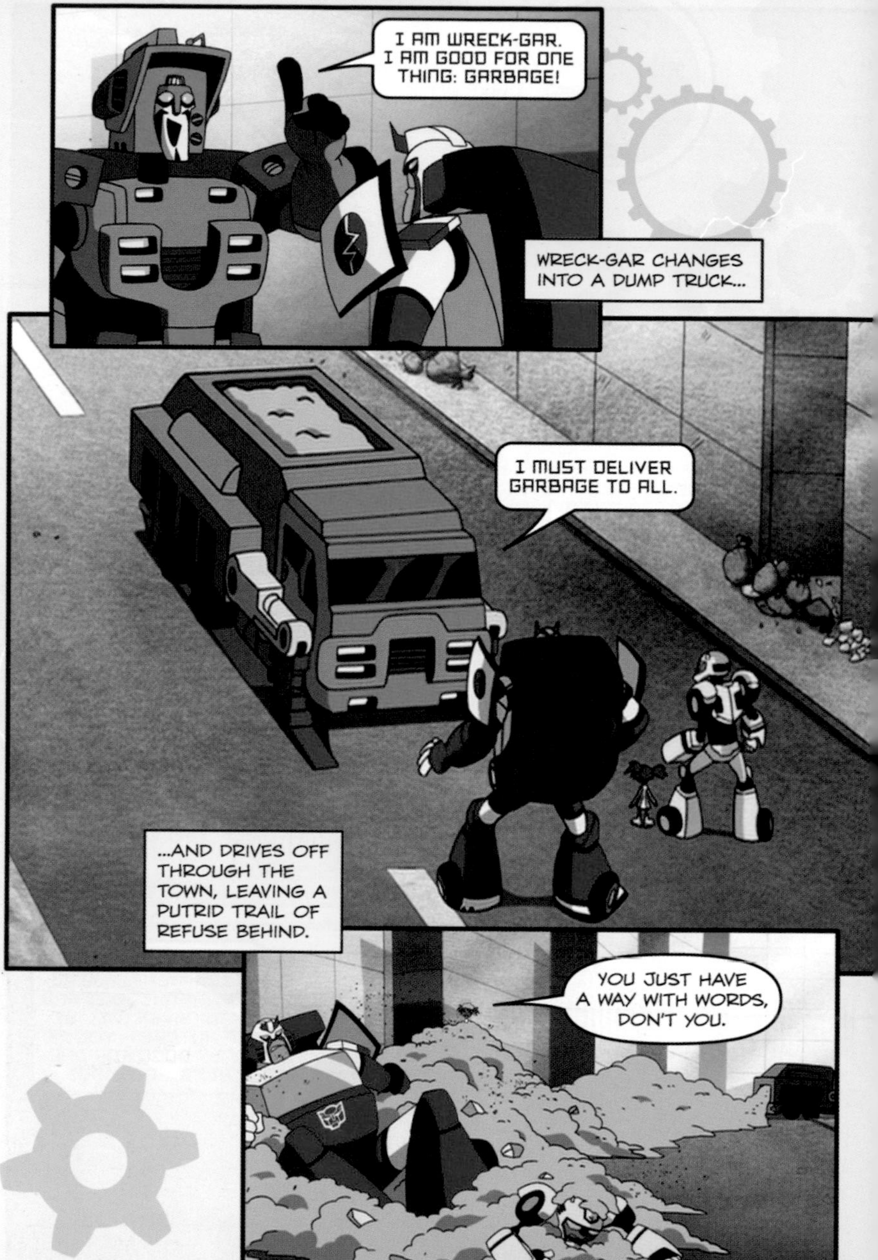
I AM WRECK-GAR. I AM GOOD FOR ONE THING: GARBAGE!
WRECK-GAR CHANGES INTO A DUMP TRUCK...
I MUST DELIVER GARBAGE TO ALL.
...AND DRIVES OFF THROUGH THE TOWN, LEAVING A PUTRID TRAIL OF REFUSE BEHIND.
YOU JUST HAVE A WAY WITH WORDS, DON'T YOU.

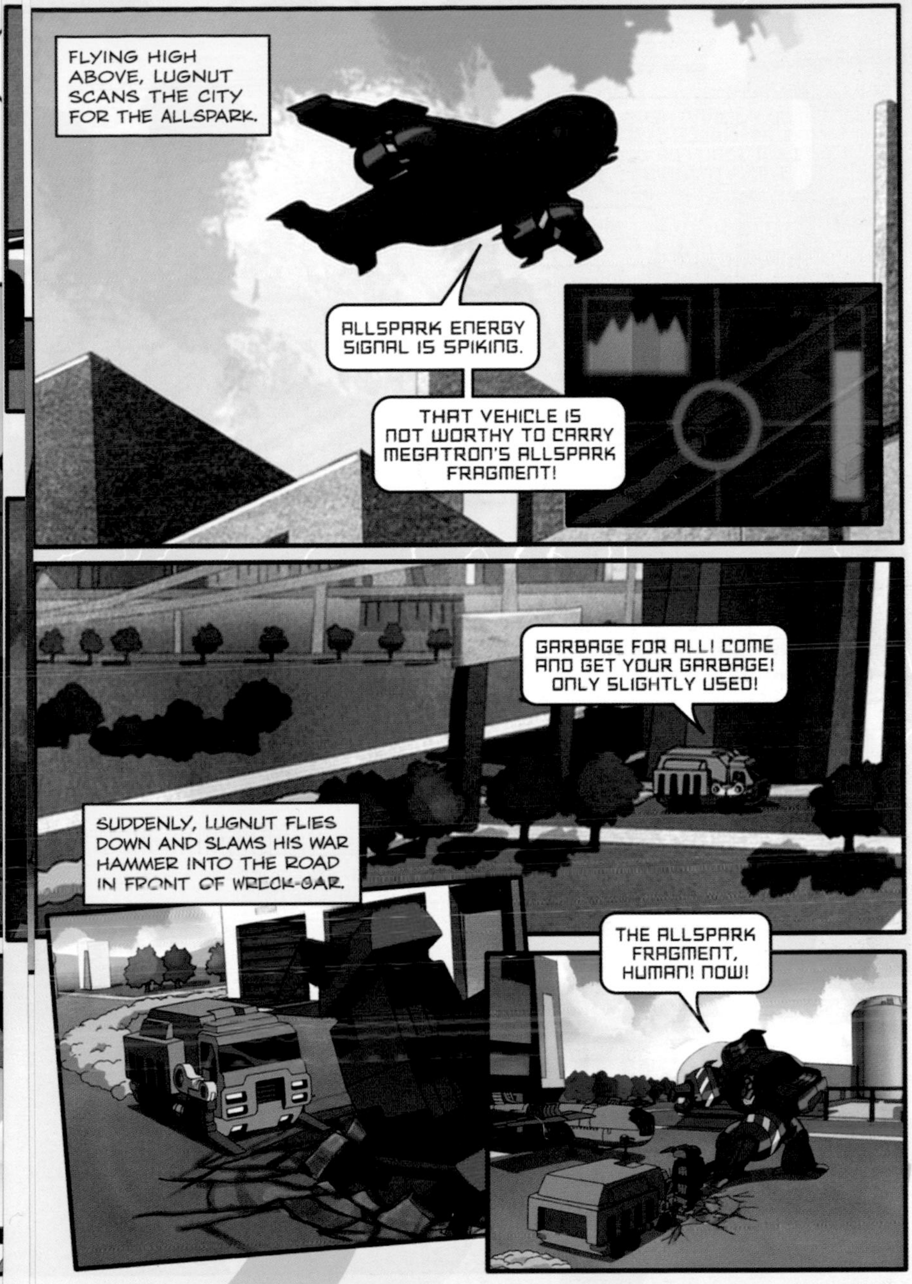
FLYING HIGH ABOVE, LUGNUT SCANS THE CITY FOR THE ALLSPARK.
ALLSPARK ENERGY SIGNAL IS SPIKING.
THAT VEHICLE IS NOT WORTHY TO CARRY MEGATRON'S ALLSPARK FRAGMENT!
GARBAGE FOR ALL! COME AND GET YOUR GARBAGE! ONLY SLIGHTLY USED!
SUDDENLY, LUGNUT FLIES DOWN AND SLAMS HIS WAR HAMMER INTO THE ROAD IN FRONT OF WRECK-GAR.
THE ALLSPARK FRAGMENT, HUMAN! NOW!

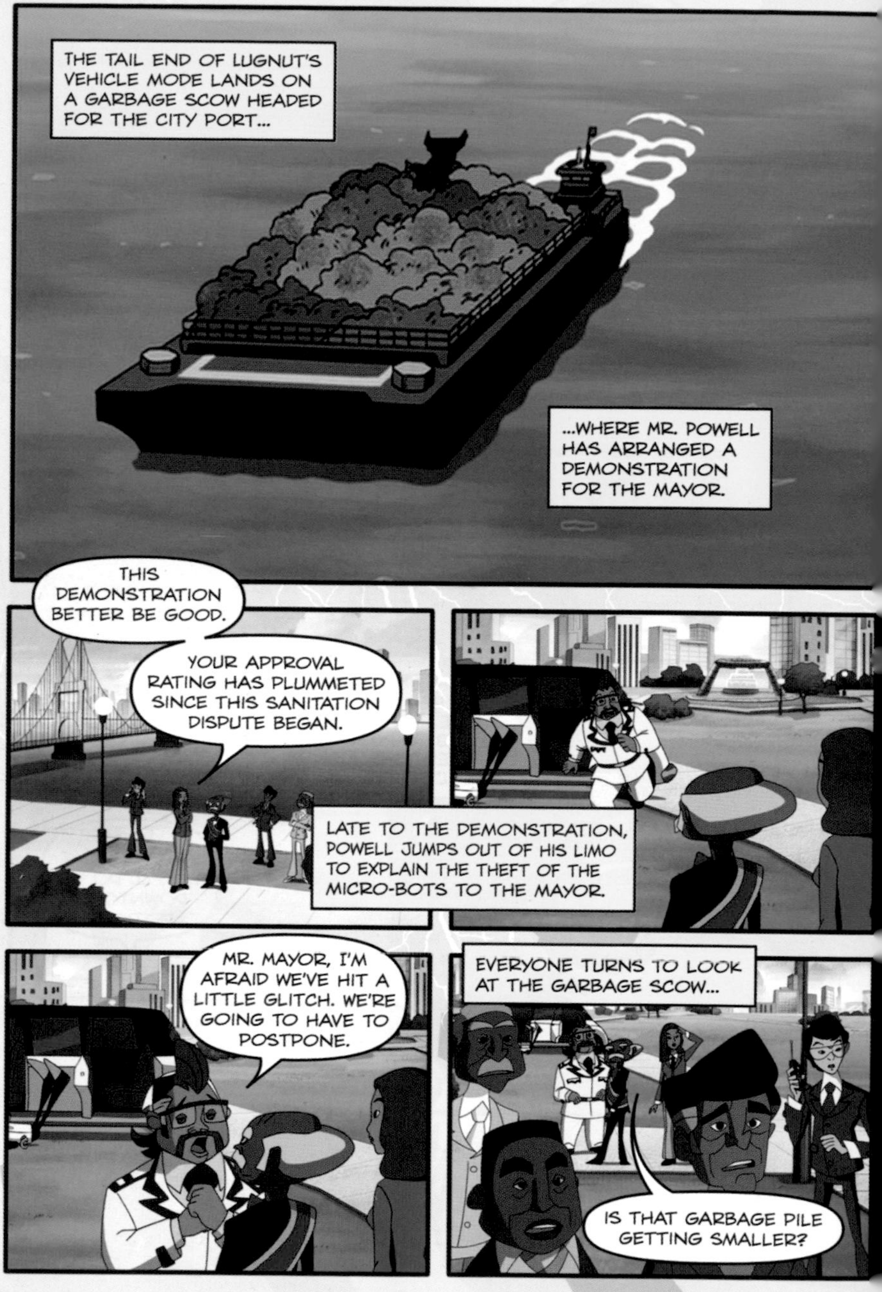
THE TAIL END OF LUGNUT'S VEHICLE MODE LANDS ON A GARBAGE SCOW HEADED FOR THE CITY PORT...
...WHERE MR. POWELL HAS ARRANGED A DEMONSTRATION FOR THE MAYOR.
THIS DEMONSTRATION BETTER BE GOOD.
YOUR APPROVAL RATING HAS PLUMMETED SINCE THIS SANITATION DISPUTE BEGAN.
LATE TO THE DEMONSTRATION, POWELL JUMPS OUT OF HIS LIMO TO EXPLAIN THE THEFT OF THE MICRO-BOTS TO THE MAYOR.
MR. MAYOR, I'M AFRAID WE'VE HIT A LITTLE GLITCH. WE'RE GOING TO HAVE TO POSTPONE.
EVERYONE TURNS TO LOOK AT THE GARBAGE SCOW...
IS THAT GARBAGE PILE GETTING SMALLER?

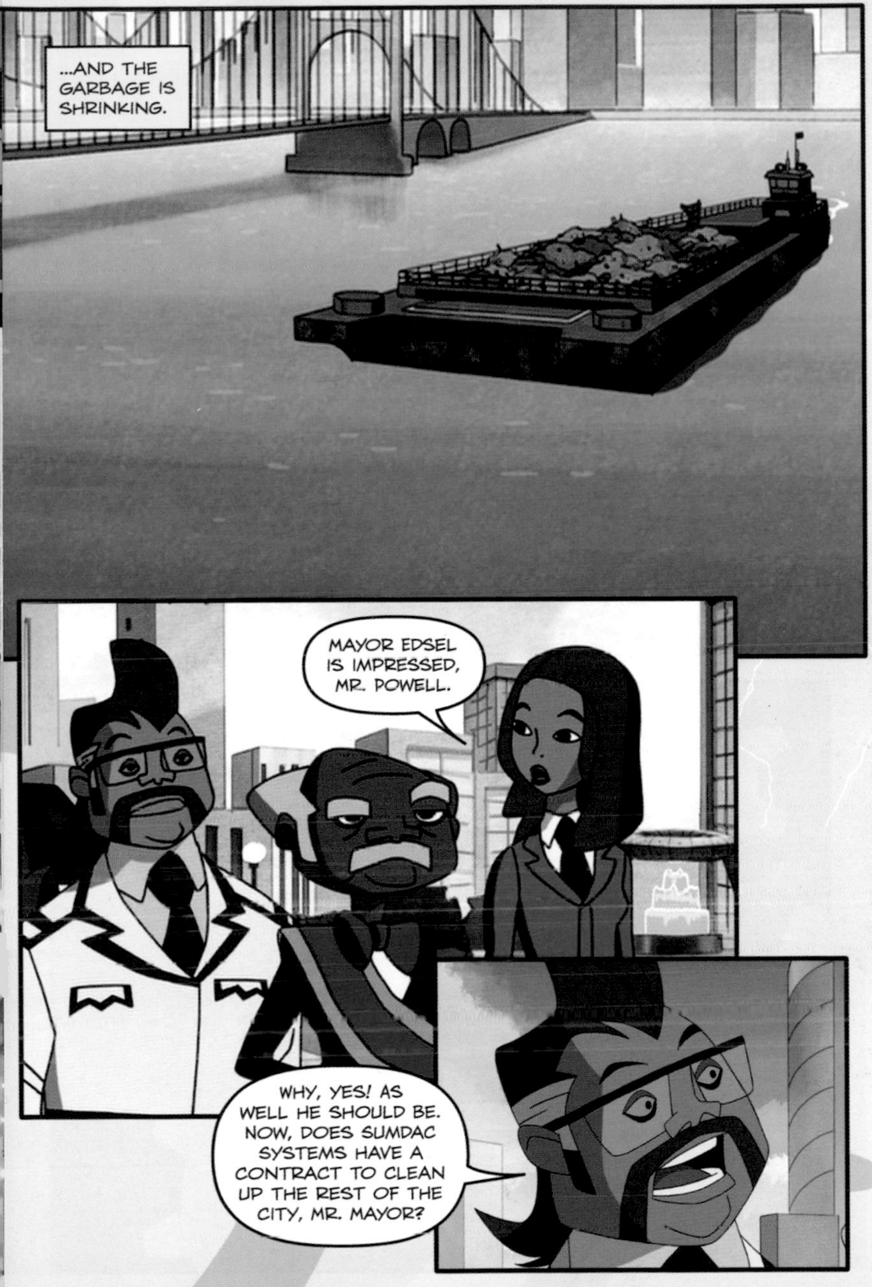

...AND THE GARBAGE IS SHRINKING.
MAYOR EDSEL IS IMPRESSED, MR. POWELL.
WHY, YES! AS WELL HE SHOULD BE. NOW, DOES SUMDAC SYSTEMS HAVE A CONTRACT TO CLEAN UP THE REST OF THE CITY, MR. MAYOR?

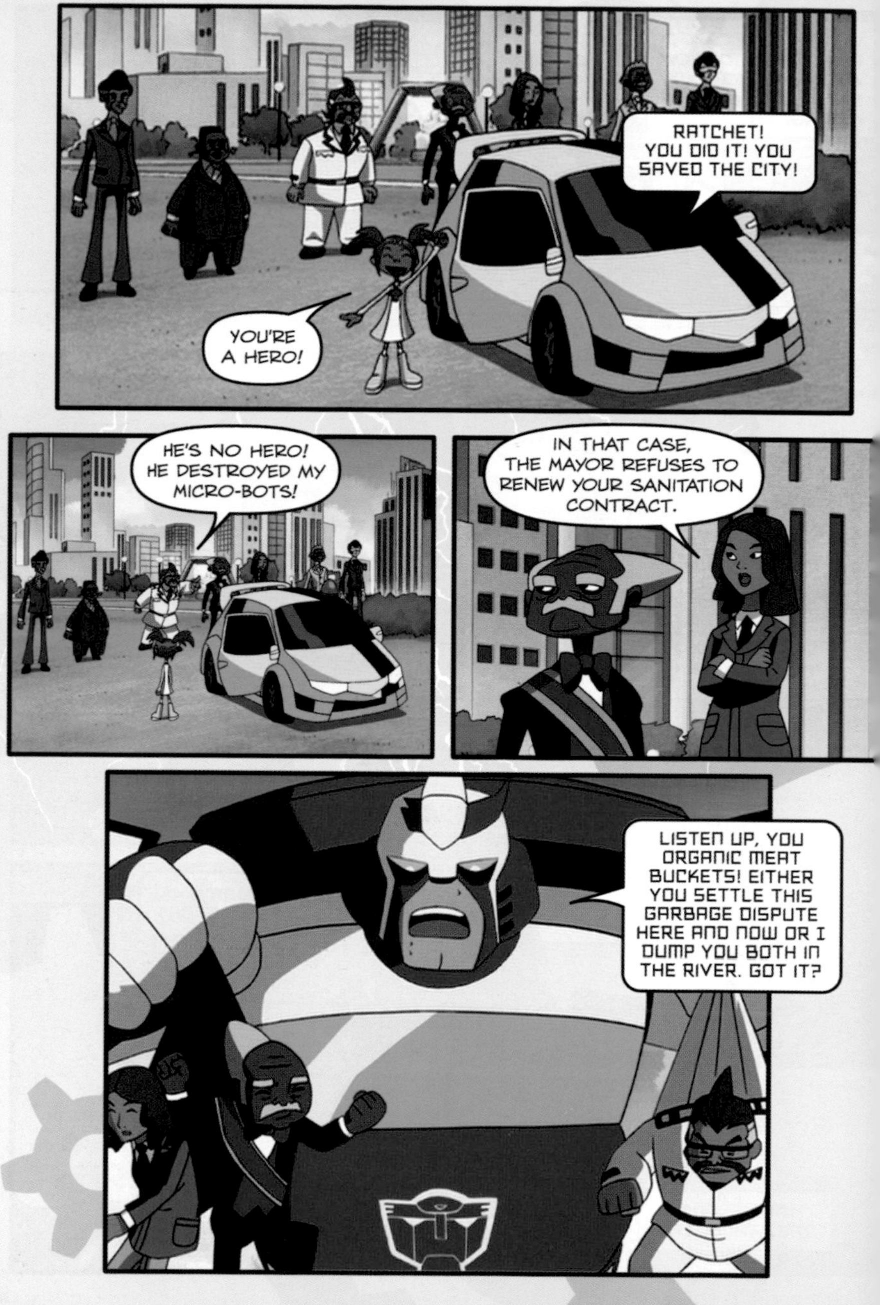
RATCHET! YOU DID IT! YOU SAVED THE CITY!
YOU'RE A HERO!
HE'S NO HERO! HE DESTROYED MY MICRO-BOTS!
IN THAT CASE, THE MAYOR REFUSES TO RENEW YOUR SANITATION CONTRACT.
LISTEN UP, YOU ORGANIC MEAT BUCKETS! EITHER YOU SETTLE THIS GARBAGE DISPUTE HERE AND NOW OR I DUMP YOU BOTH IN THE RIVER. GOT IT?

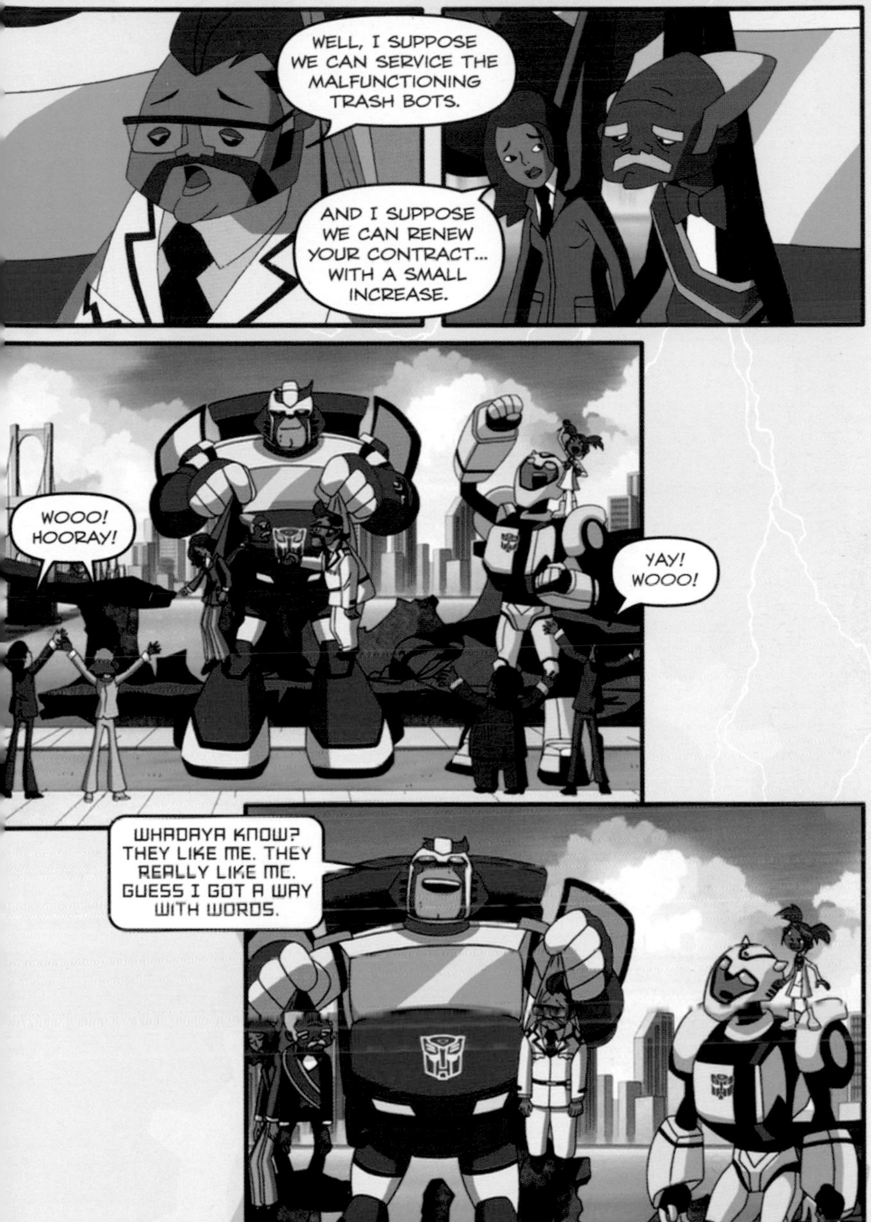
WELL, I SUPPOSE WE CAN SERVICE THE MALFUNCTIONING TRASH BOTS.
AND I SUPPOSE WE CAN RENEW YOUR CONTRACT... WITH A SMALL INCREASE.
WOOO! HOORAY!
YAY! WOOO!
WHADAYA KNOW? THEY LIKE ME. THEY REALLY LIKE ME. GUESS I GOT A WAY WITH WORDS.

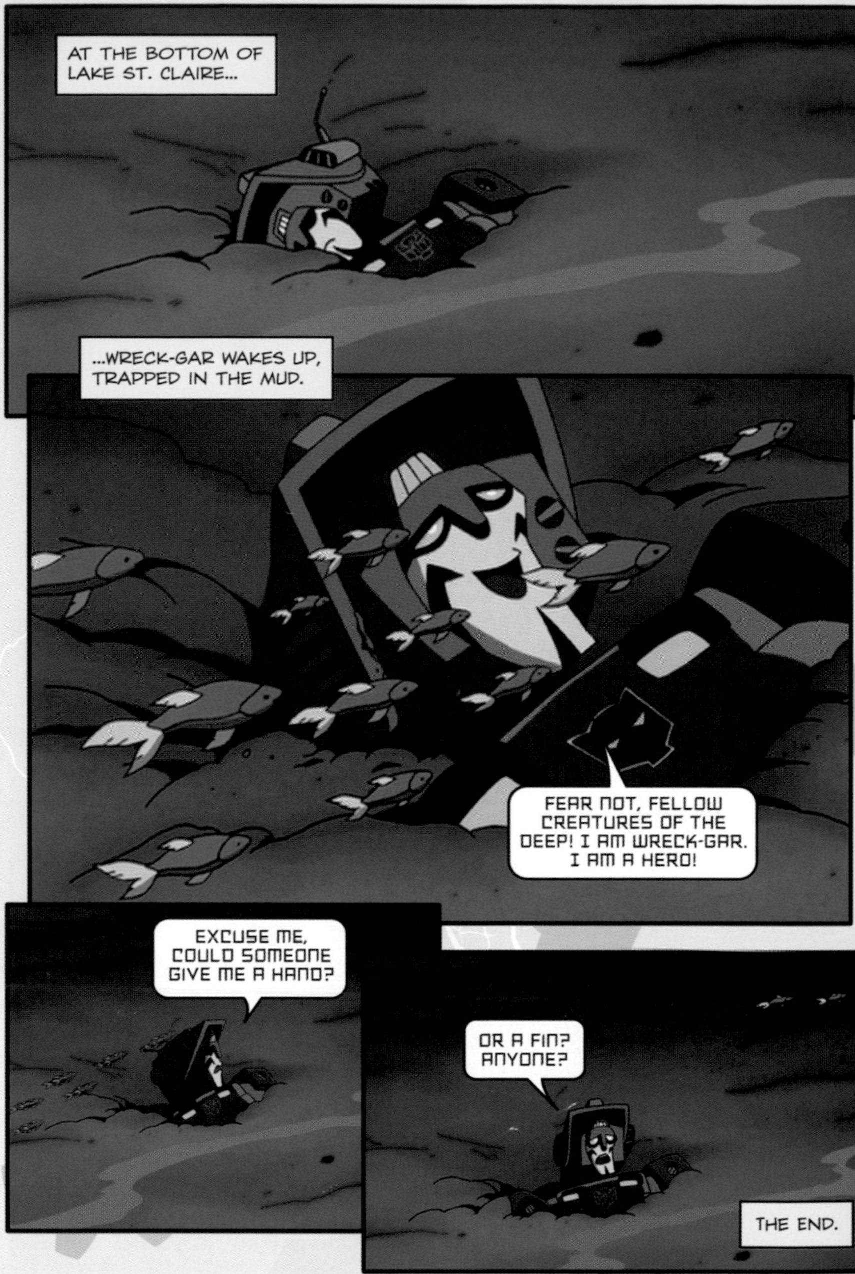
AT THE BOTTOM OF LAKE ST. CLAIRE...
...WRECK-GAR WAKES UP, TRAPPED IN THE MUD.
FEAR NOT, FELLOW CREATURES OF THE DEEP! I AM WRECK-GAR. I AM A HERO!
EXCUSE ME, COULD SOMEONE GIVE ME A HAND?
OR A FIN? ANYONE?
THE END.

VELOCITY

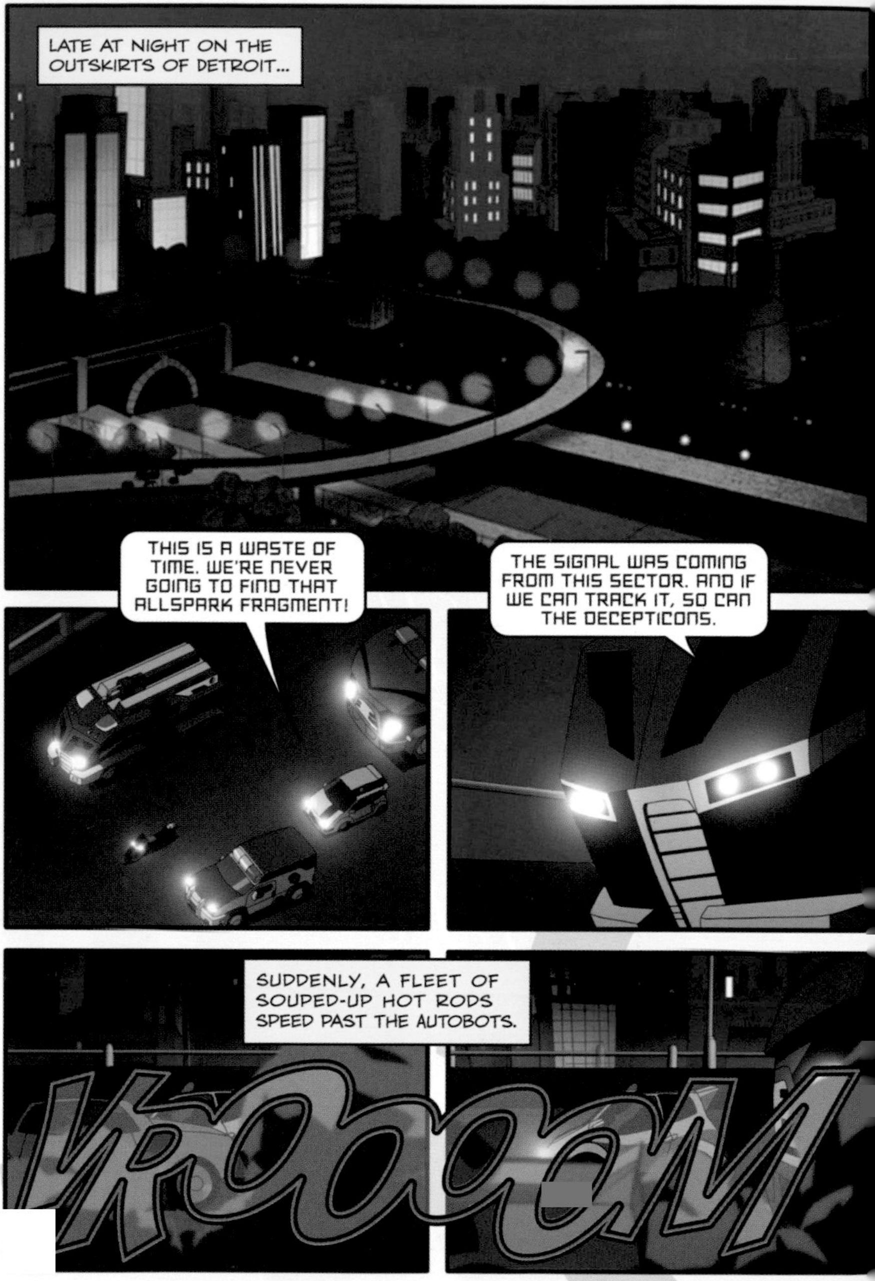
LATE AT NIGHT ON THE OUTSKIRTS OF DETROIT...
THIS IS A WASTE OF TIME. WE'RE NEVER GOING TO FIND THAT ALLSPARK FRAGMENT!
THE SIGNAL WAS COMING FROM THIS SECTOR. AND IF WE CAN TRACK IT, SO CAN THE DECEPTICONS.
SUDDENLY, A FLEET OF SOUPED-UP HOT RODS SPEED PAST THE AUTOBOTS.
VROOOOM

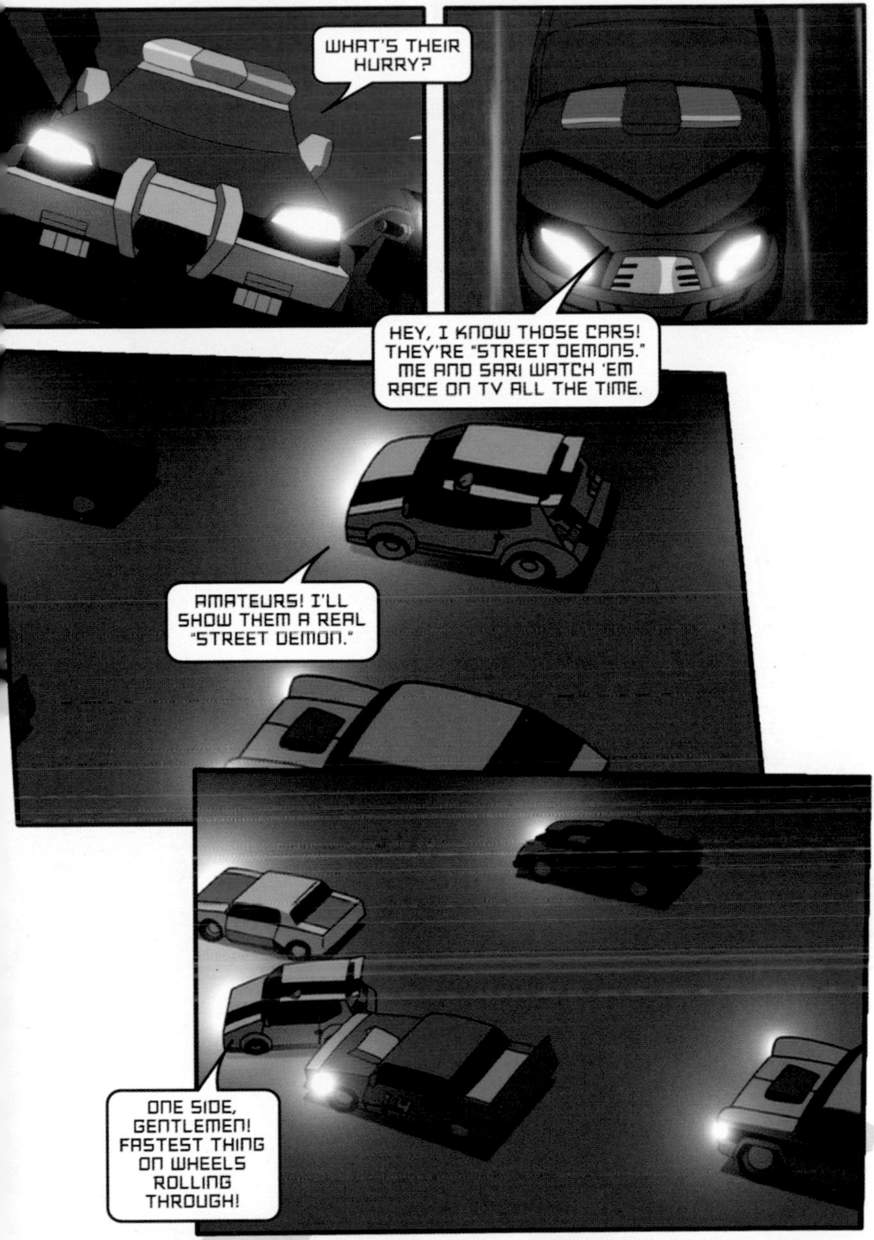
WHAT'S THEIR HURRY?
HEY, I KNOW THOSE CARS! THEY'RE "STREET DEMONS." ME AND SARI WATCH 'EM RACE ON TV ALL THE TIME.
AMATEURS! I'LL SHOW THEM A REAL "STREET DEMON."
ONE SIDE, GENTLEMEN! FASTEST THING ON WHEELS ROLLING THROUGH!

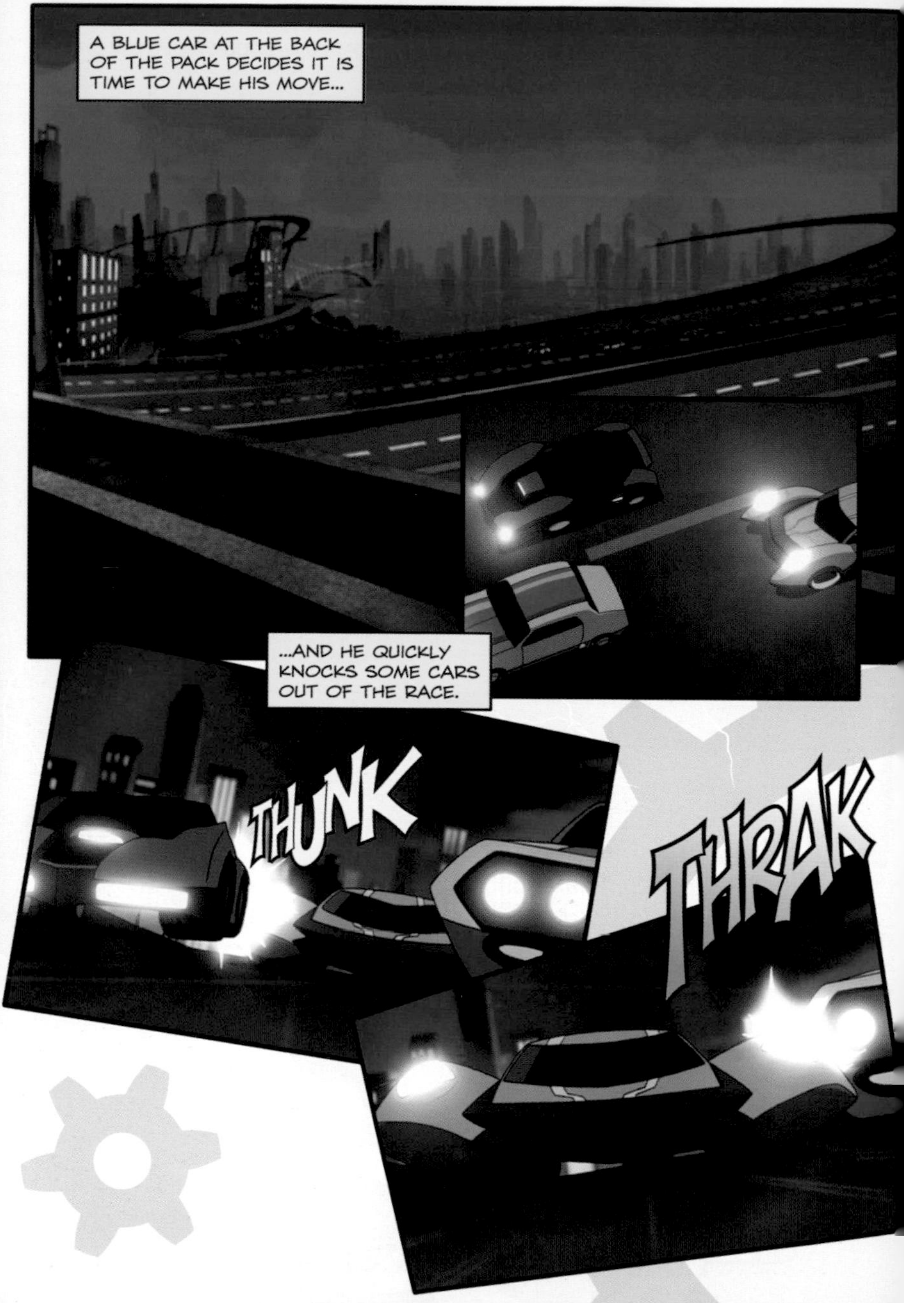
A BLUE CAR AT THE BACK OF THE PACK DECIDES IT IS TIME TO MAKE HIS MOVE...
...AND HE QUICKLY KNOCKS SOME CARS OUT OF THE RACE.
THUNK
THRAK

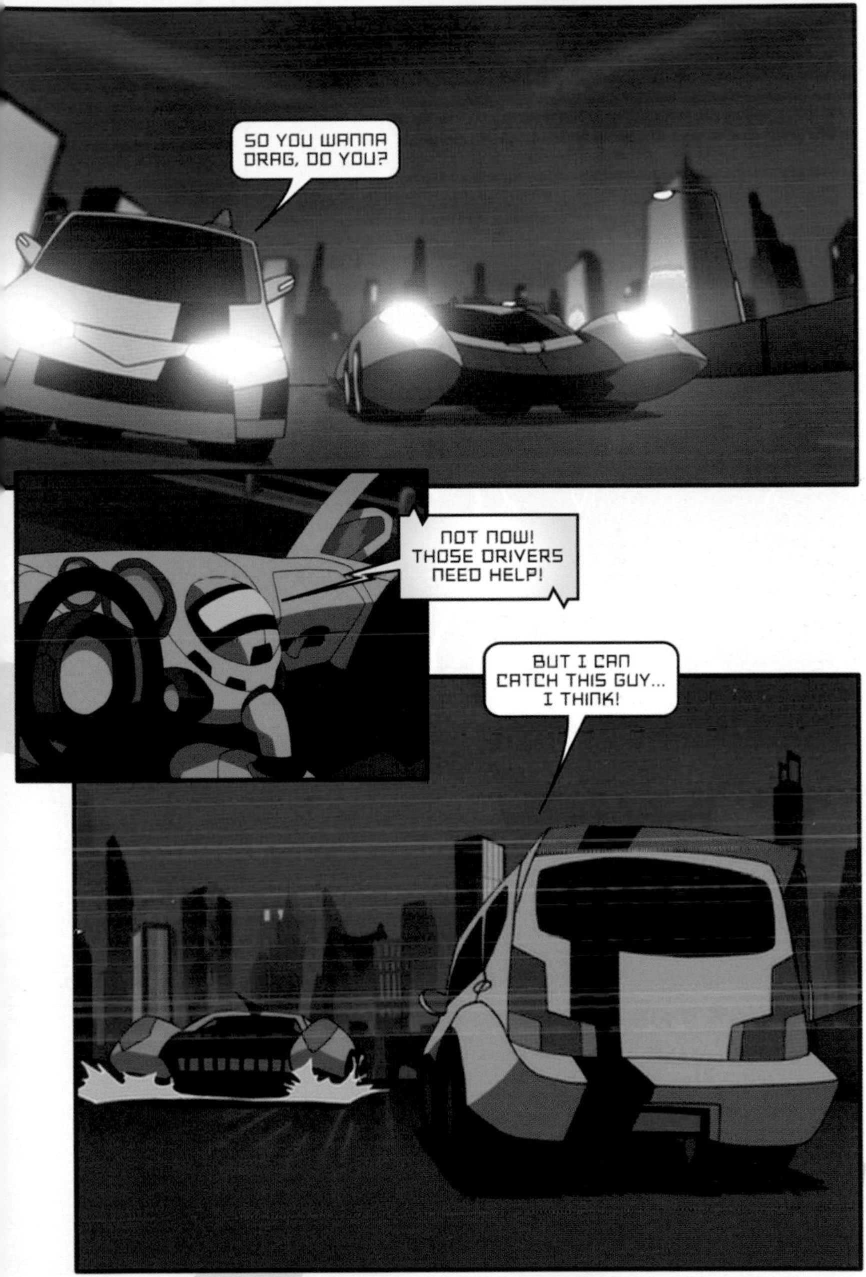
SO YOU WANNA DRAG, DO YOU?
NOT NOW! THOSE DRIVERS NEED HELP!
BUT I CAN CATCH THIS GUY... I THINK!

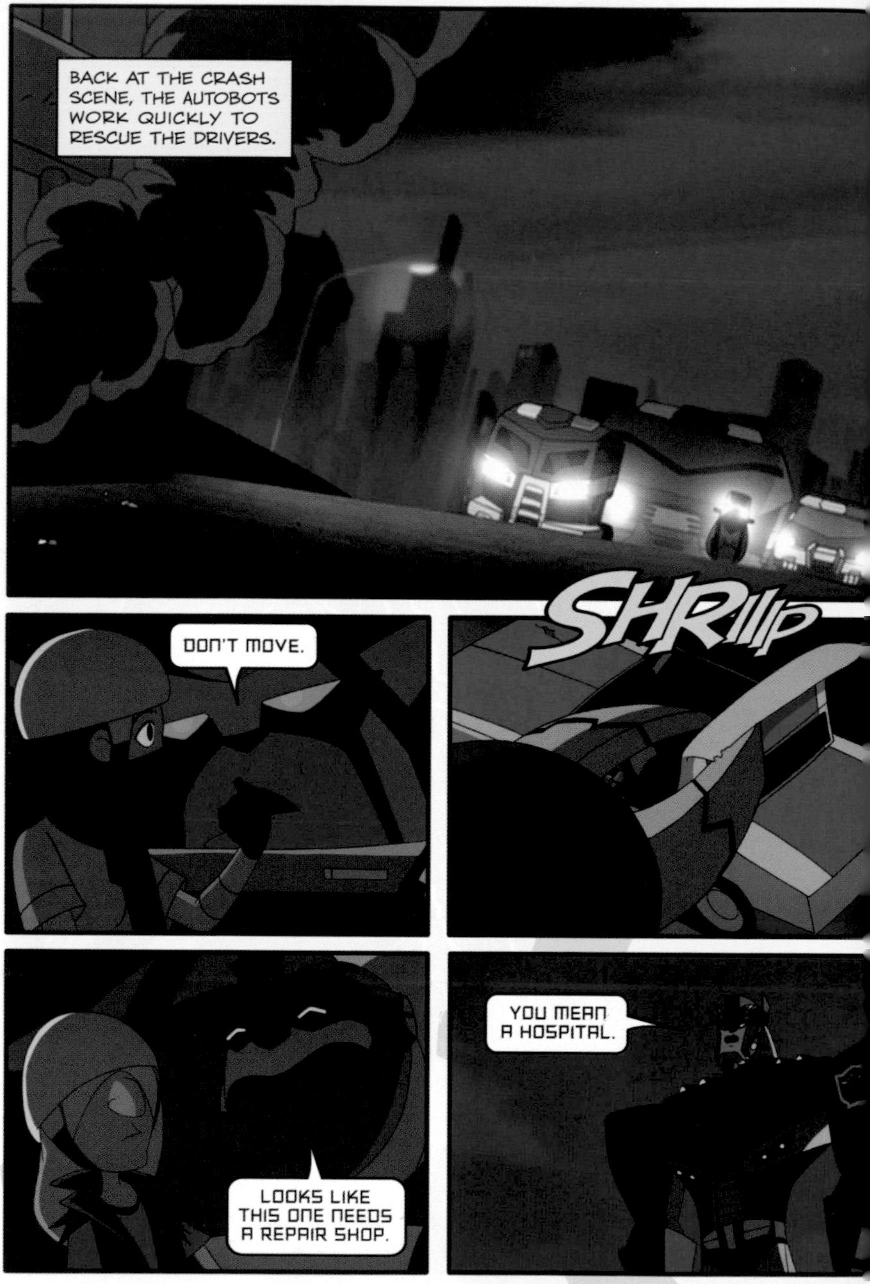
BACK AT THE CRASH SCENE, THE AUTOBOTS WORK QUICKLY TO RESCUE THE DRIVERS.
DON'T MOVE.
SHRIIP
LOOKS LIKE THIS ONE NEEDS A REPAIR SHOP.
YOU MEAN A HOSPITAL.

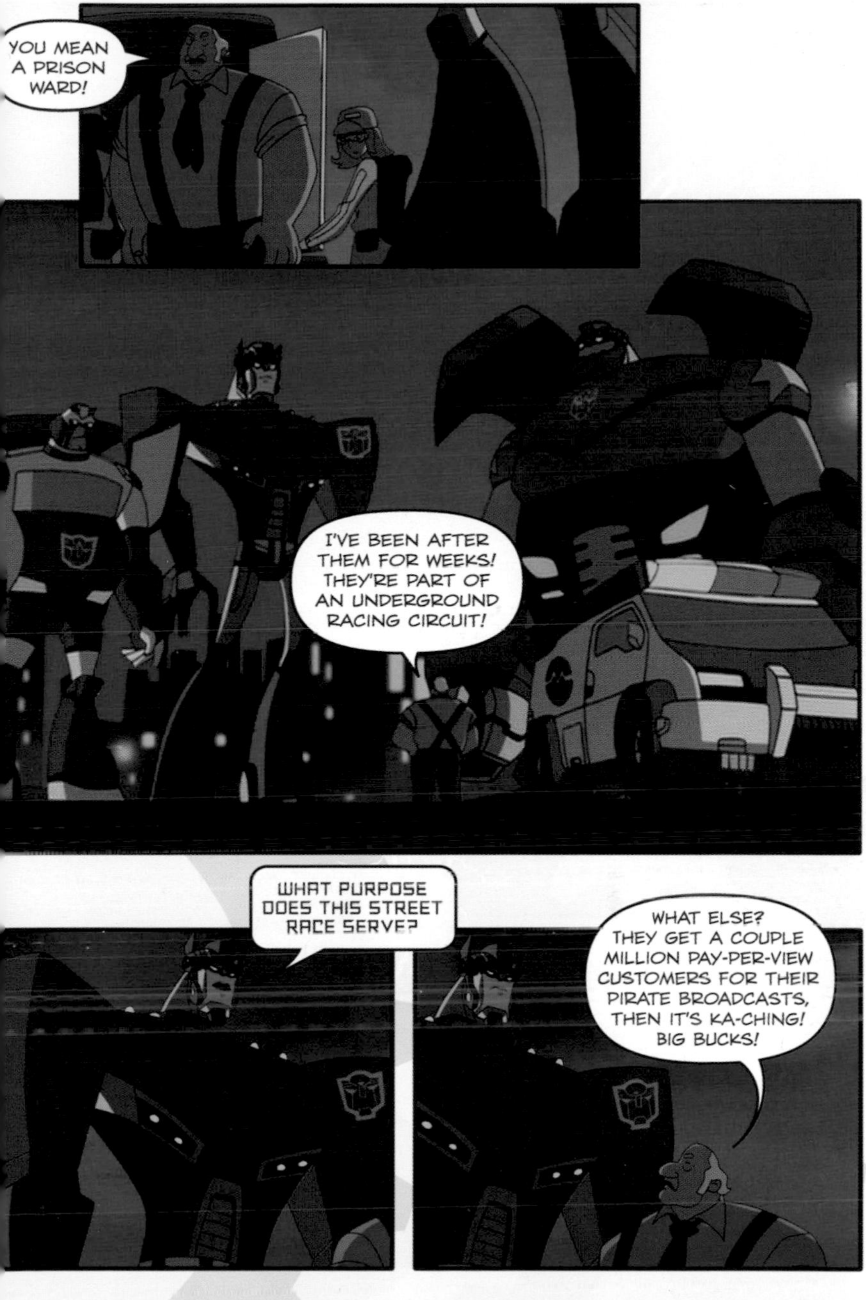
YOU MEAN A PRISON WARD!
I'VE BEEN AFTER THEM FOR WEEKS! THEY'RE PART OF AN UNDERGROUND RACING CIRCUIT!
WHAT PURPOSE DOES THIS STREET RACE SERVE?
WHAT ELSE? THEY GET A COUPLE MILLION PAY-PER-VIEW CUSTOMERS FOR THEIR PIRATE BROADCASTS, THEN IT'S KA-CHING! BIG BUCKS!

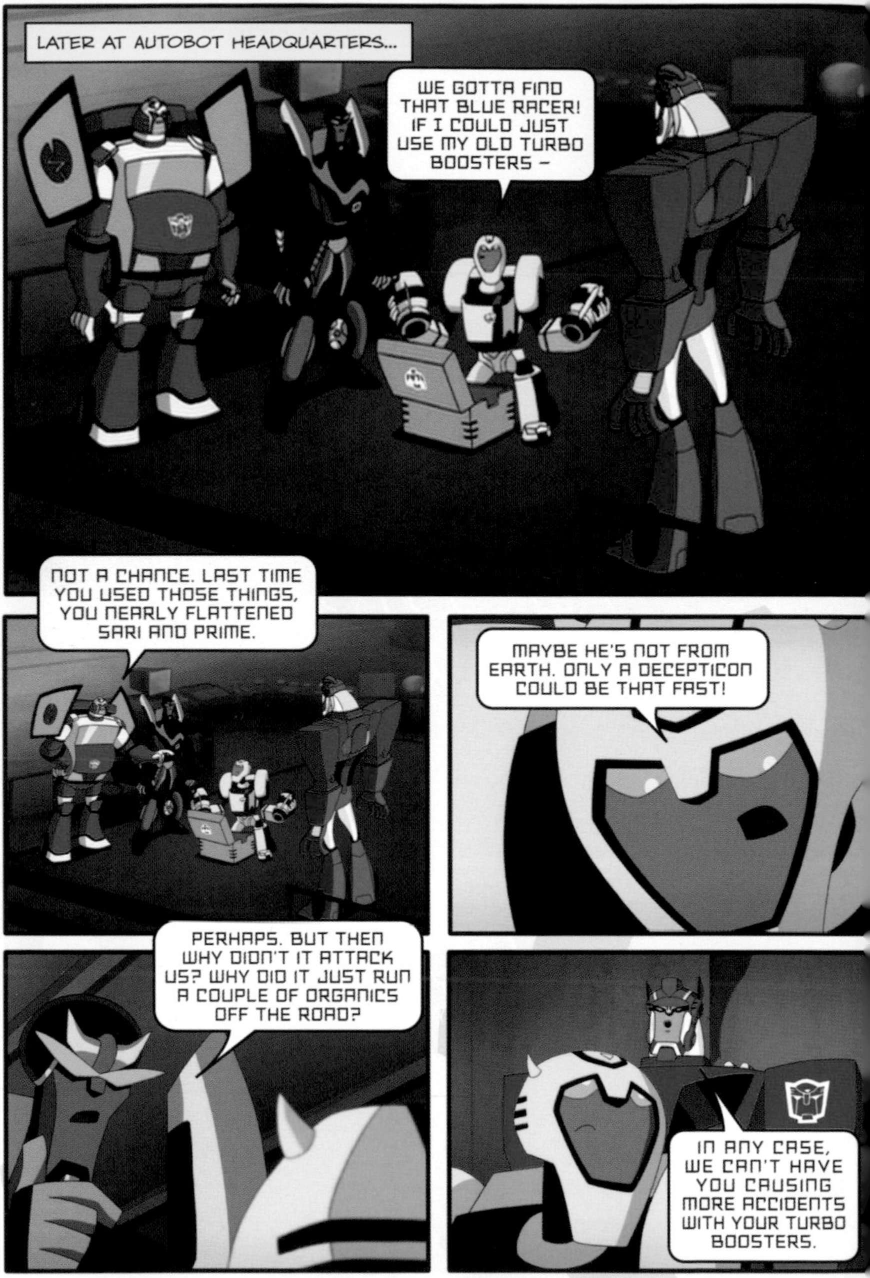
LATER AT AUTOBOT HEADQUARTERS...
WE GOTTA FIND THAT BLUE RACER! IF I COULD JUST USE MY OLD TURBO BOOSTERS –
NOT A CHANCE. LAST TIME YOU USED THOSE THINGS, YOU NEARLY FLATTENED SARI AND PRIME.
MAYBE HE'S NOT FROM EARTH. ONLY A DECEPTICON COULD BE THAT FAST!
PERHAPS. BUT THEN WHY DIDN'T IT ATTACK US? WHY DID IT JUST RUN A COUPLE OF ORGANICS OFF THE ROAD?
IN ANY CASE, WE CAN'T HAVE YOU CAUSING MORE ACCIDENTS WITH YOUR TURBO BOOSTERS.

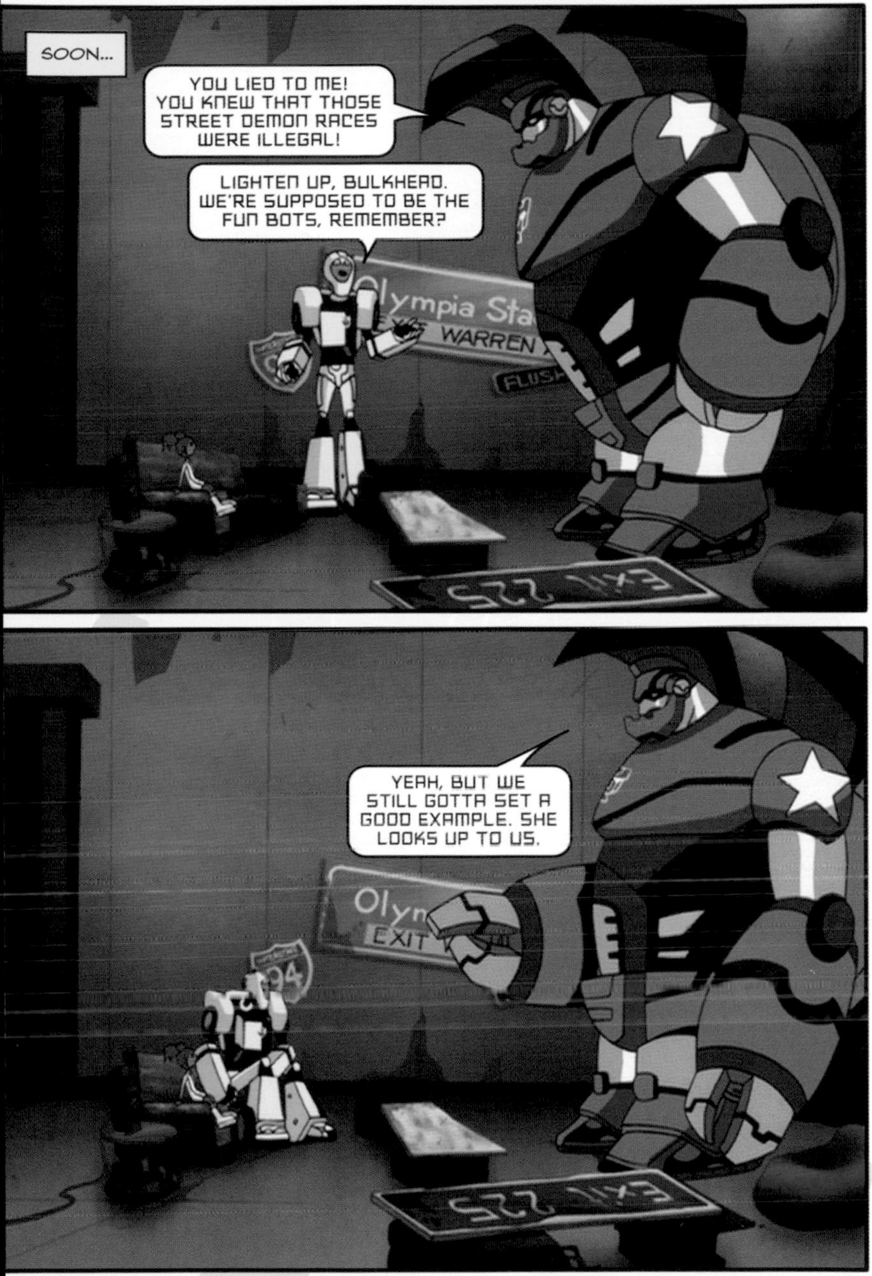
SOON...
YOU LIED TO ME! YOU KNEW THAT THOSE STREET DEMON RACES WERE ILLEGAL!
LIGHTEN UP, BULKHEAD. WE'RE SUPPOSED TO BE THE FUN BOTS, REMEMBER?
YEAH, BUT WE STILL GOTTA SET A GOOD EXAMPLE. SHE LOOKS UP TO US.

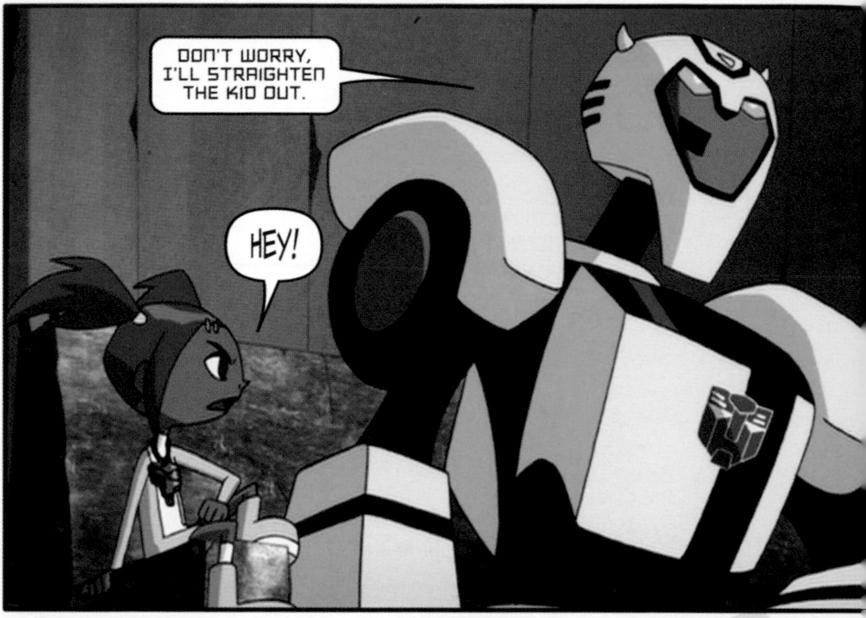
DON'T WORRY, I'LL STRAIGHTEN THE KID OUT.
HEY!

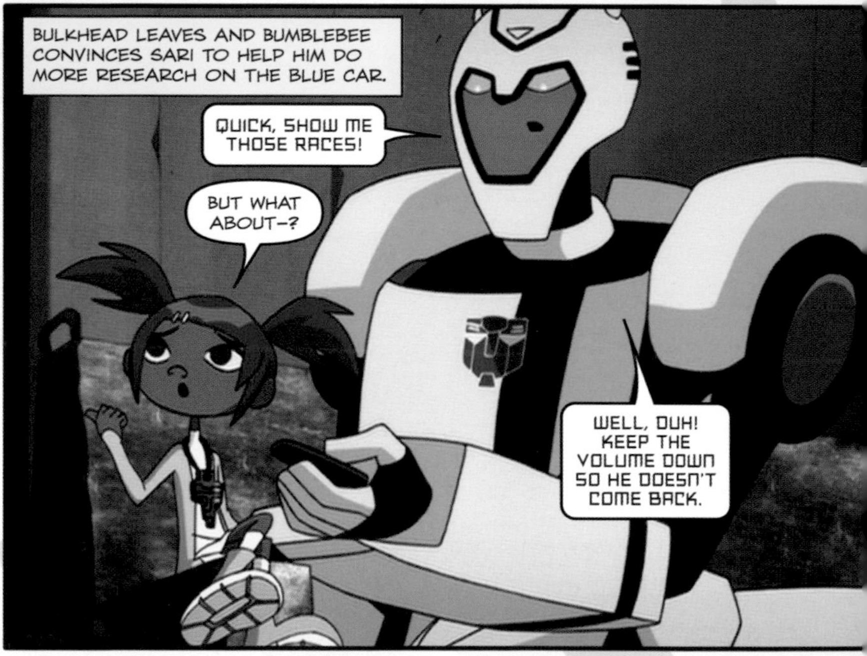
BULKHEAD LEAVES AND BUMBLEBEE CONVINCES SARI TO HELP HIM DO MORE RESEARCH ON THE BLUE CAR.
QUICK, SHOW ME THOSE RACES!
BUT WHAT ABOUT–?
WELL, DUH! KEEP THE VOLUME DOWN SO HE DOESN'T COME BACK.

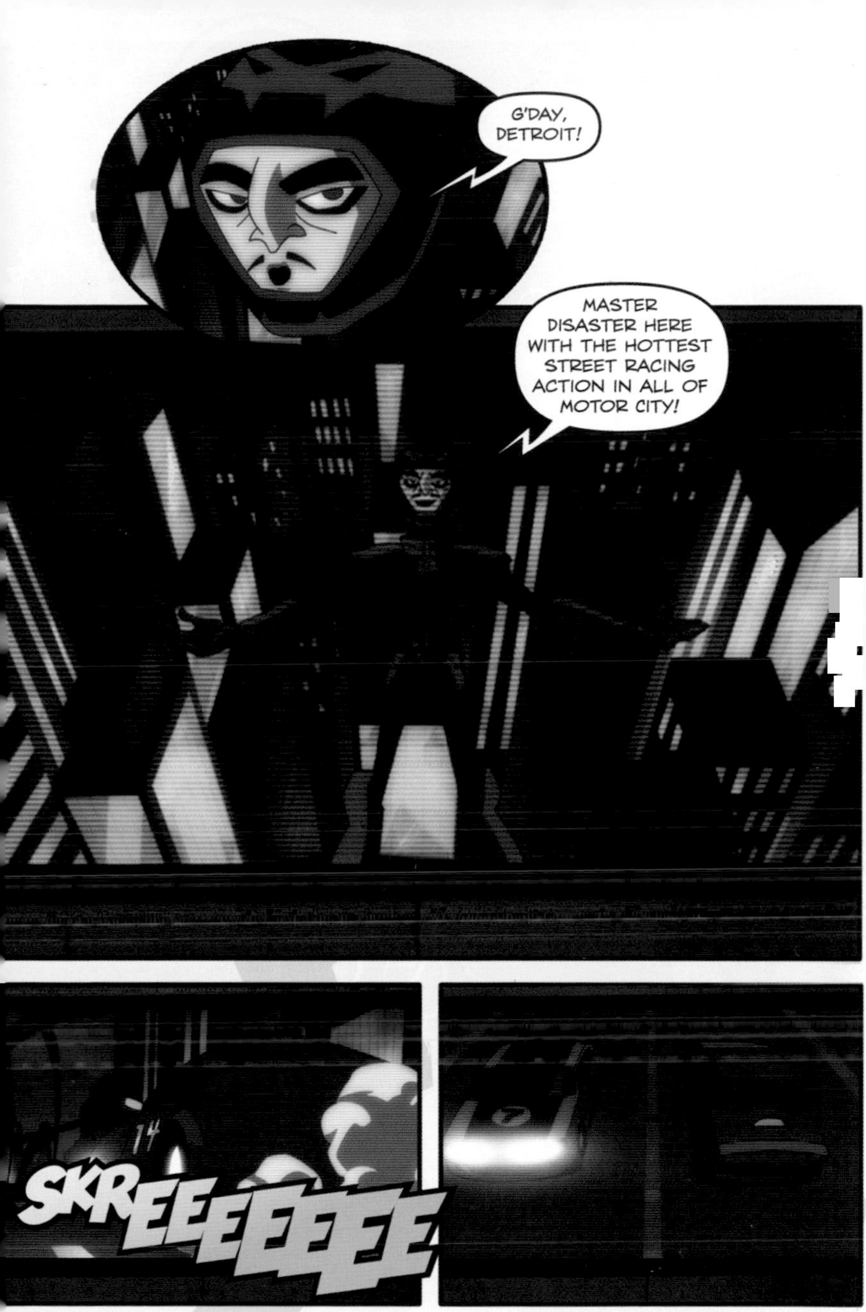
G'DAY, DETROIT!
MASTER DISASTER HERE WITH THE HOTTEST STREET RACING ACTION IN ALL OF MOTOR CITY!
SKREEEEEEEE

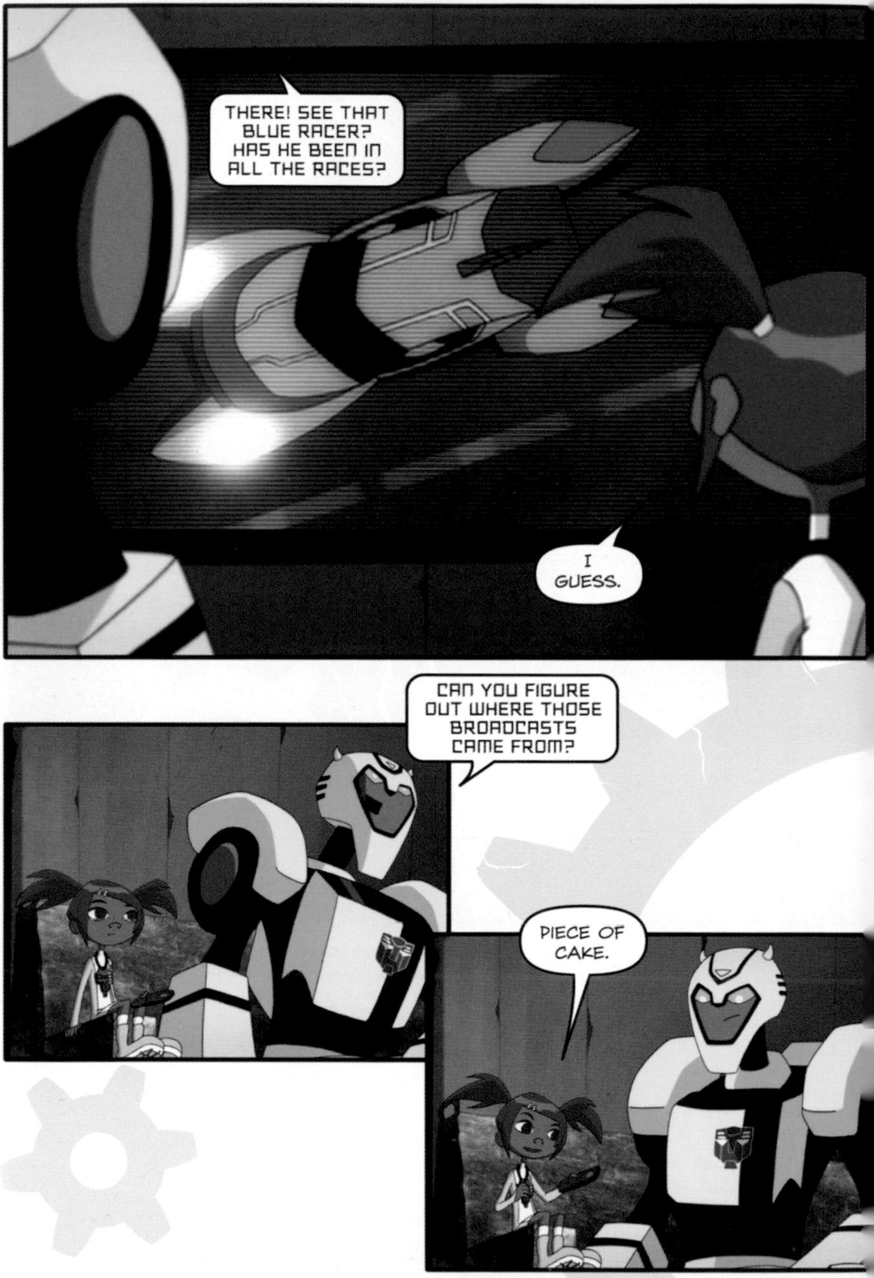
THERE! SEE THAT BLUE RACER? HAS HE BEEN IN ALL THE RACES?
I GUESS.
CAN YOU FIGURE OUT WHERE THOSE BROADCASTS CAME FROM?
PIECE OF CAKE.

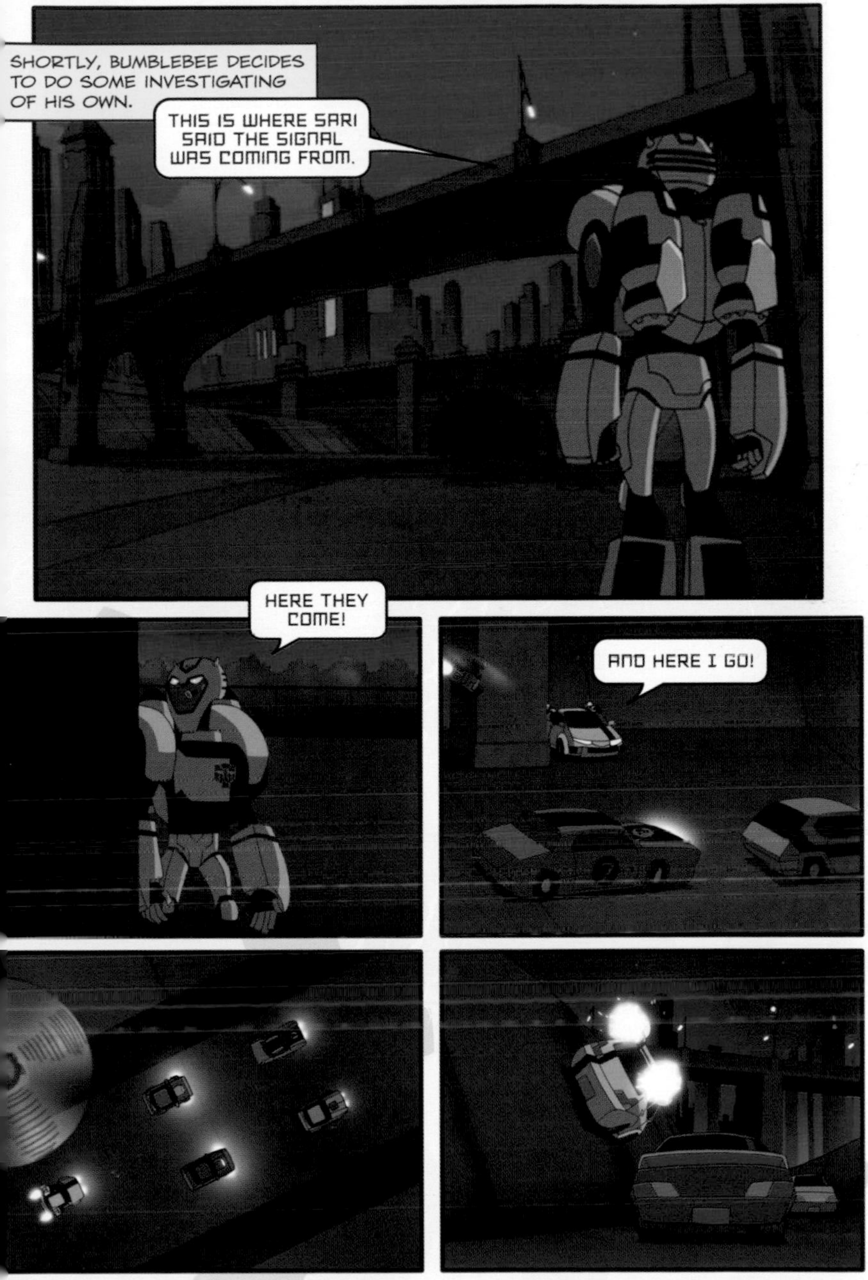
SHORTLY, BUMBLEBEE DECIDES TO DO SOME INVESTIGATING OF HIS OWN.
THIS IS WHERE SARI SAID THE SIGNAL WAS COMING FROM.
HERE THEY COME!
AND HERE I GO!

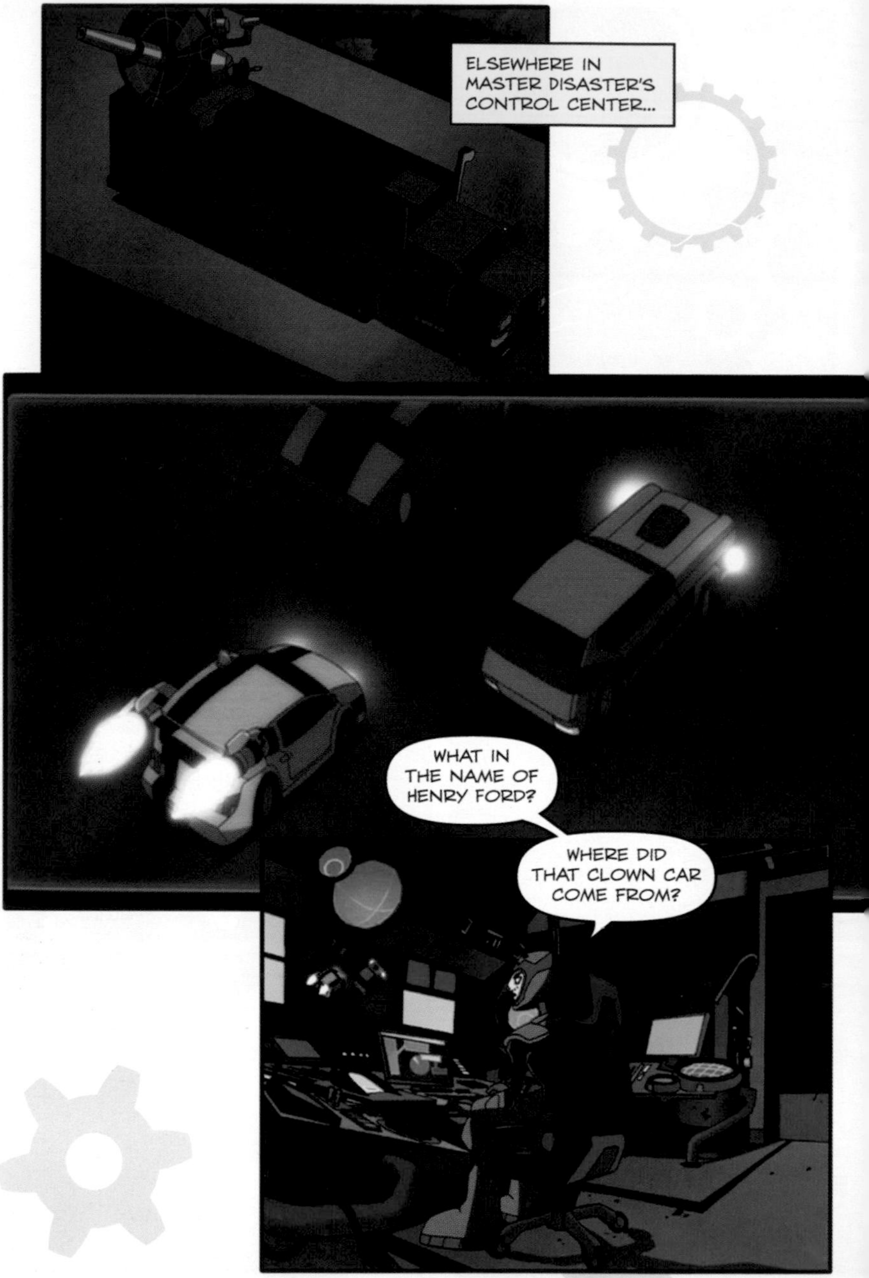
ELSEWHERE IN MASTER DISASTER'S CONTROL CENTER...
WHAT IN THE NAME OF HENRY FORD?
WHERE DID THAT CLOWN CAR COME FROM?

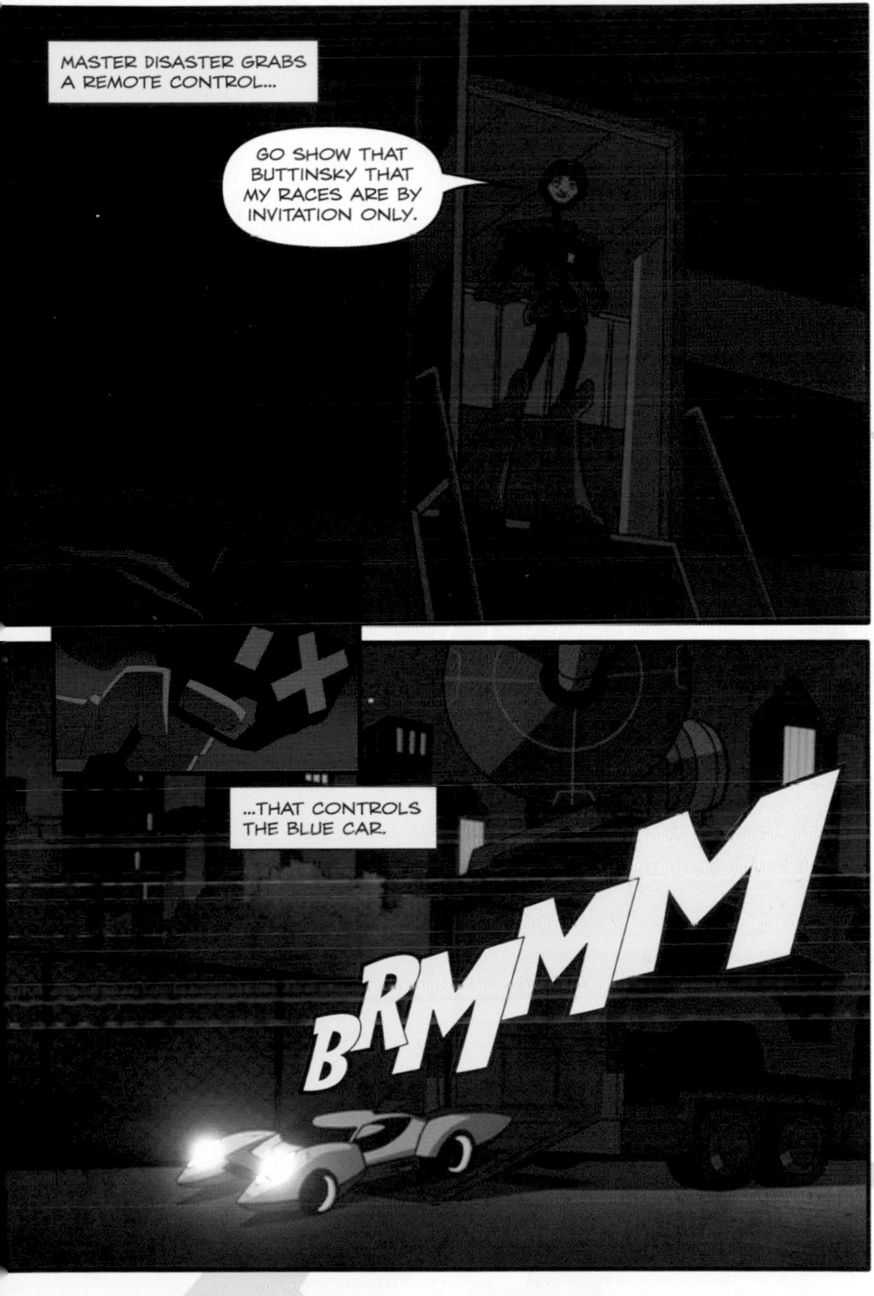
MASTER DISASTER GRABS A REMOTE CONTROL...
GO SHOW THAT BUTTINSKY THAT MY RACES ARE BY INVITATION ONLY.
...THAT CONTROLS THE BLUE CAR.
BRMMMM

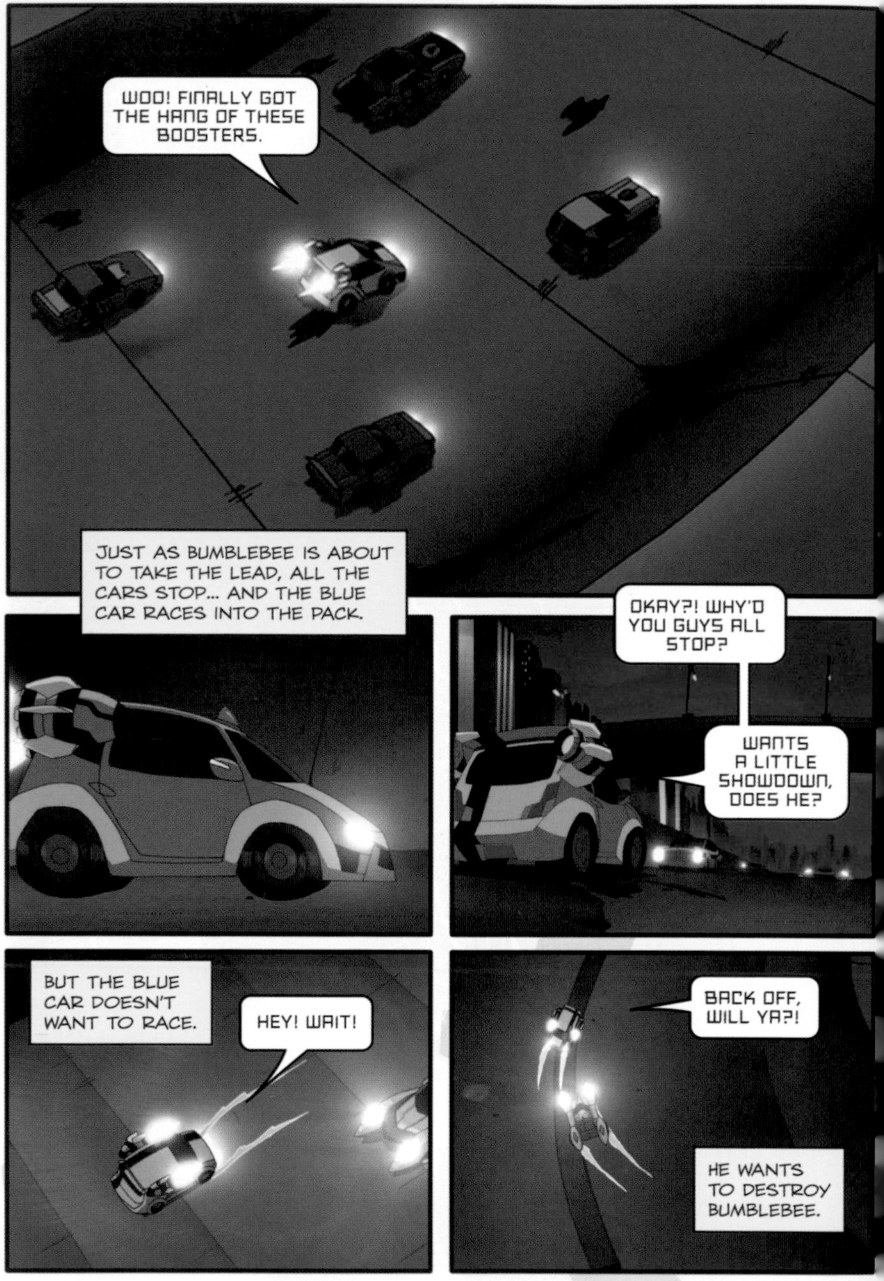
WOO! FINALLY GOT THE HANG OF THESE BOOSTERS.
JUST AS BUMBLEBEE IS ABOUT TO TAKE THE LEAD, ALL THE CARS STOP... AND THE BLUE CAR RACES INTO THE PACK.
OKAY?! WHY'D YOU GUYS ALL STOP?
WANTS A LITTLE SHOWDOWN, DOES HE?
BUT THE BLUE CAR DOESN'T WANT TO RACE.
HEY! WAIT!
BACK OFF, WILL YA?!
HE WANTS TO DESTROY BUMBLEBEE.

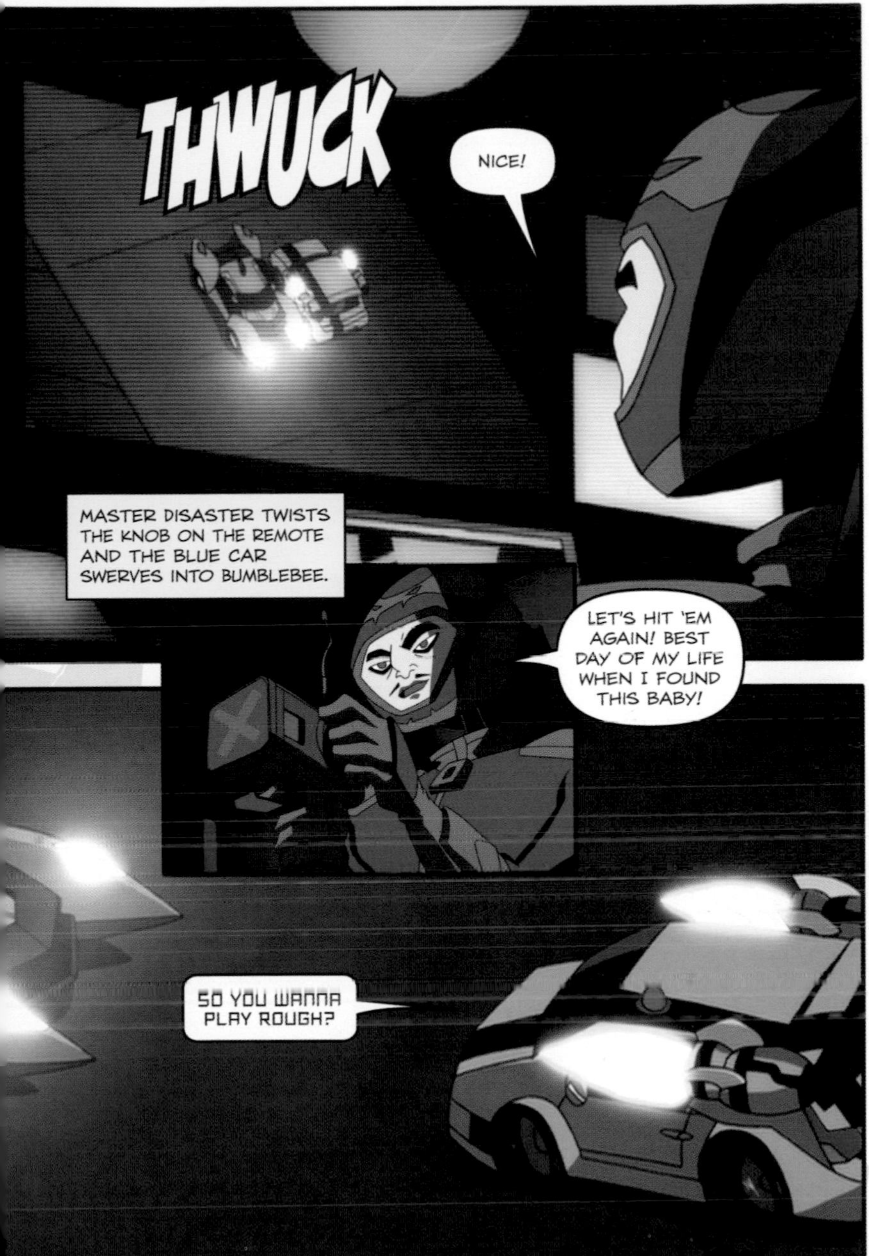
THWUCK
NICE!
MASTER DISASTER TWISTS THE KNOB ON THE REMOTE AND THE BLUE CAR SWERVES INTO BUMBLEBEE.
LET'S HIT 'EM AGAIN! BEST DAY OF MY LIFE WHEN I FOUND THIS BABY!
SO YOU WANNA PLAY ROUGH?

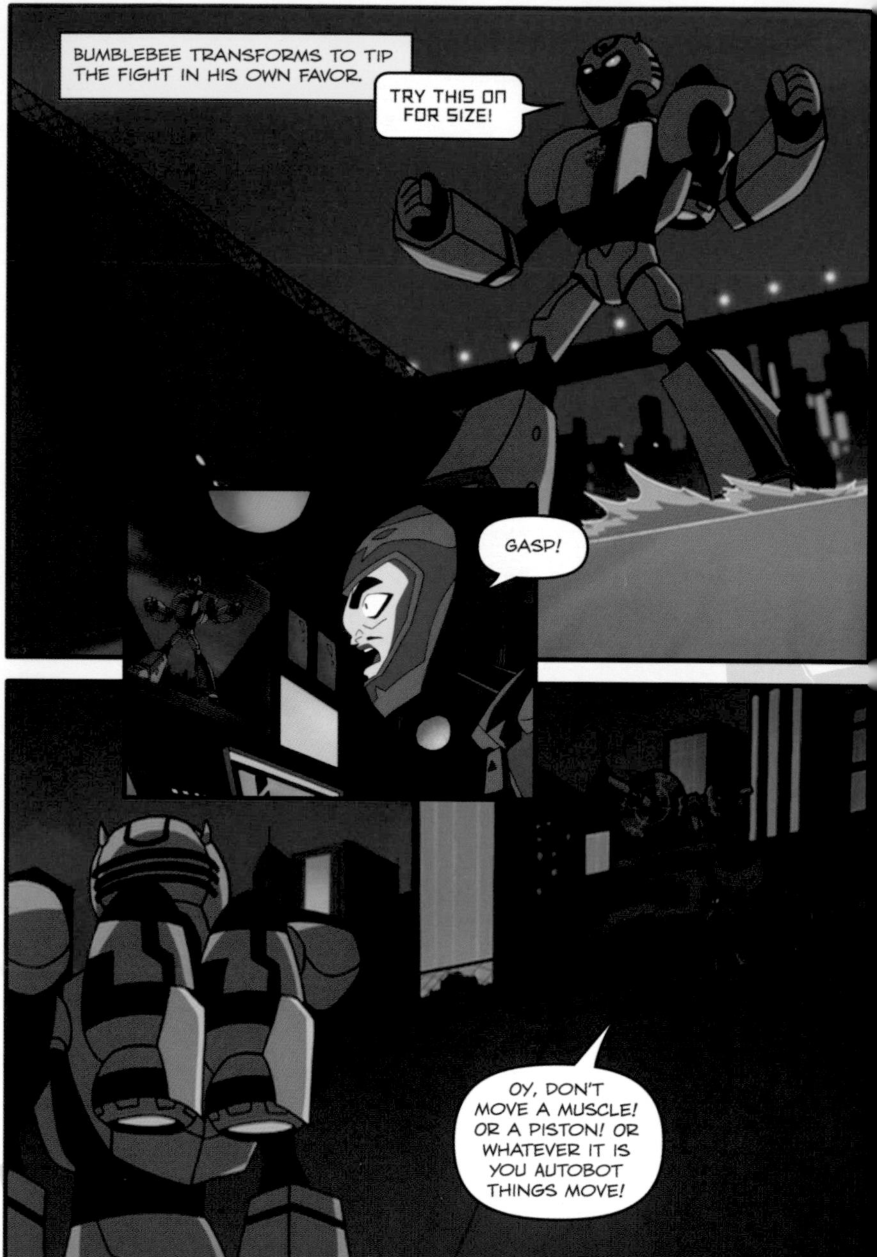
BUMBLEBEE TRANSFORMS TO TIP THE FIGHT IN HIS OWN FAVOR.
TRY THIS ON FOR SIZE!
GASP!
OY, DON'T MOVE A MUSCLE! OR A PISTON! OR WHATEVER IT IS YOU AUTOBOT THINGS MOVE!

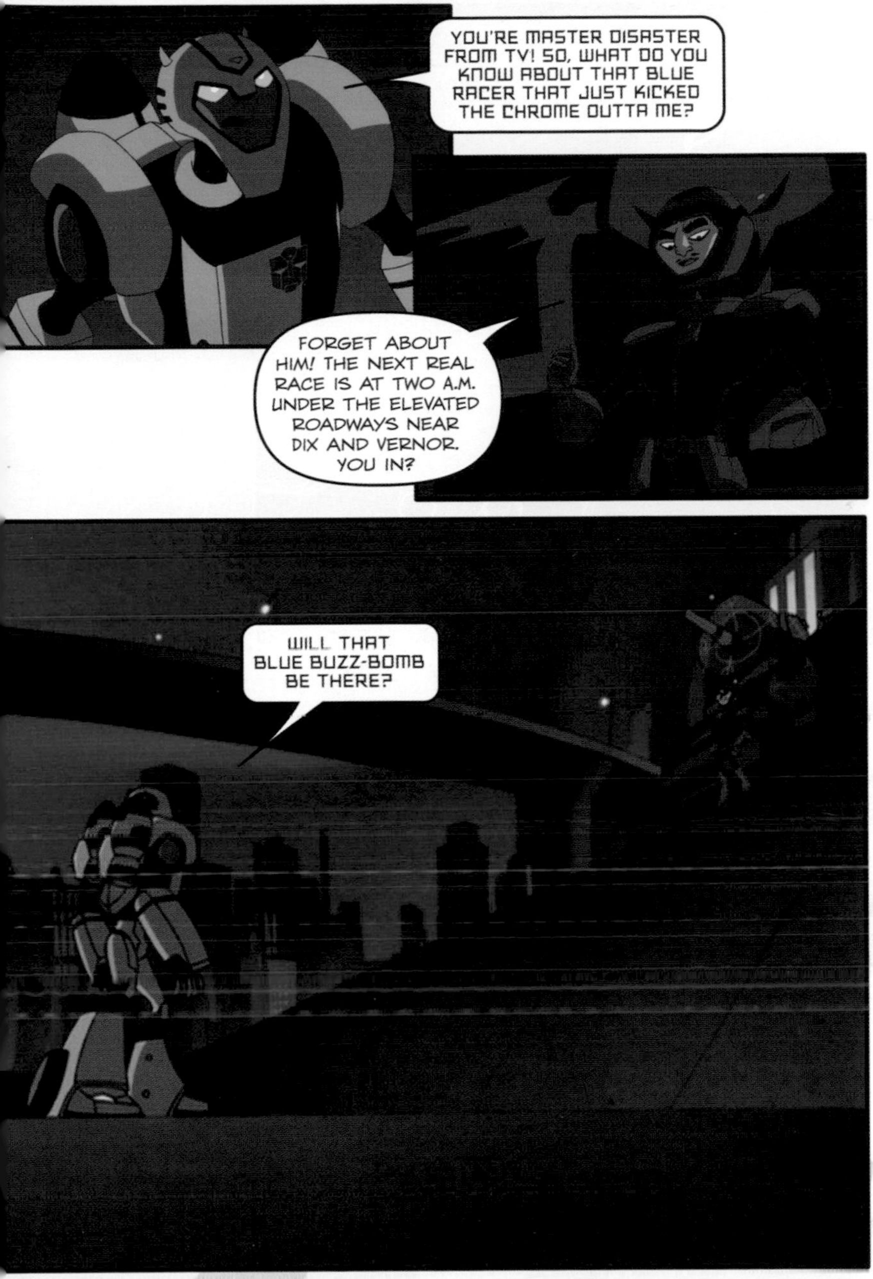

YOU'RE MASTER DISASTER FROM TV! SO, WHAT DO YOU KNOW ABOUT THAT BLUE RACER THAT JUST KICKED THE CHROME OUTTA ME?
FORGET ABOUT HIM! THE NEXT REAL RACE IS AT TWO A.M. UNDER THE ELEVATED ROADWAYS NEAR DIX AND VERNOR. YOU IN?
WILL THAT BLUE BUZZ-BOMB BE THERE?

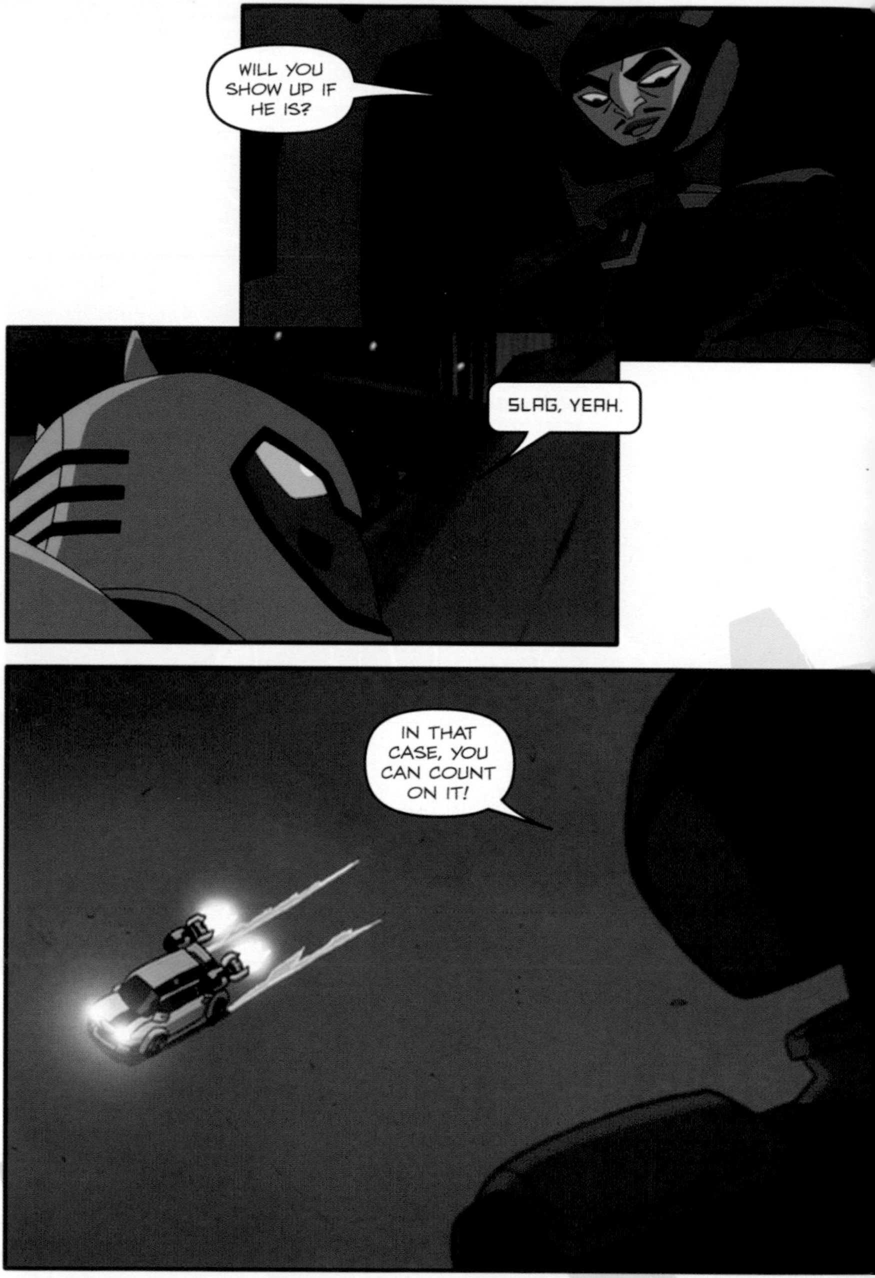

WILL YOU SHOW UP IF HE IS?
SLAG, YEAH.
IN THAT CASE, YOU CAN COUNT ON IT!

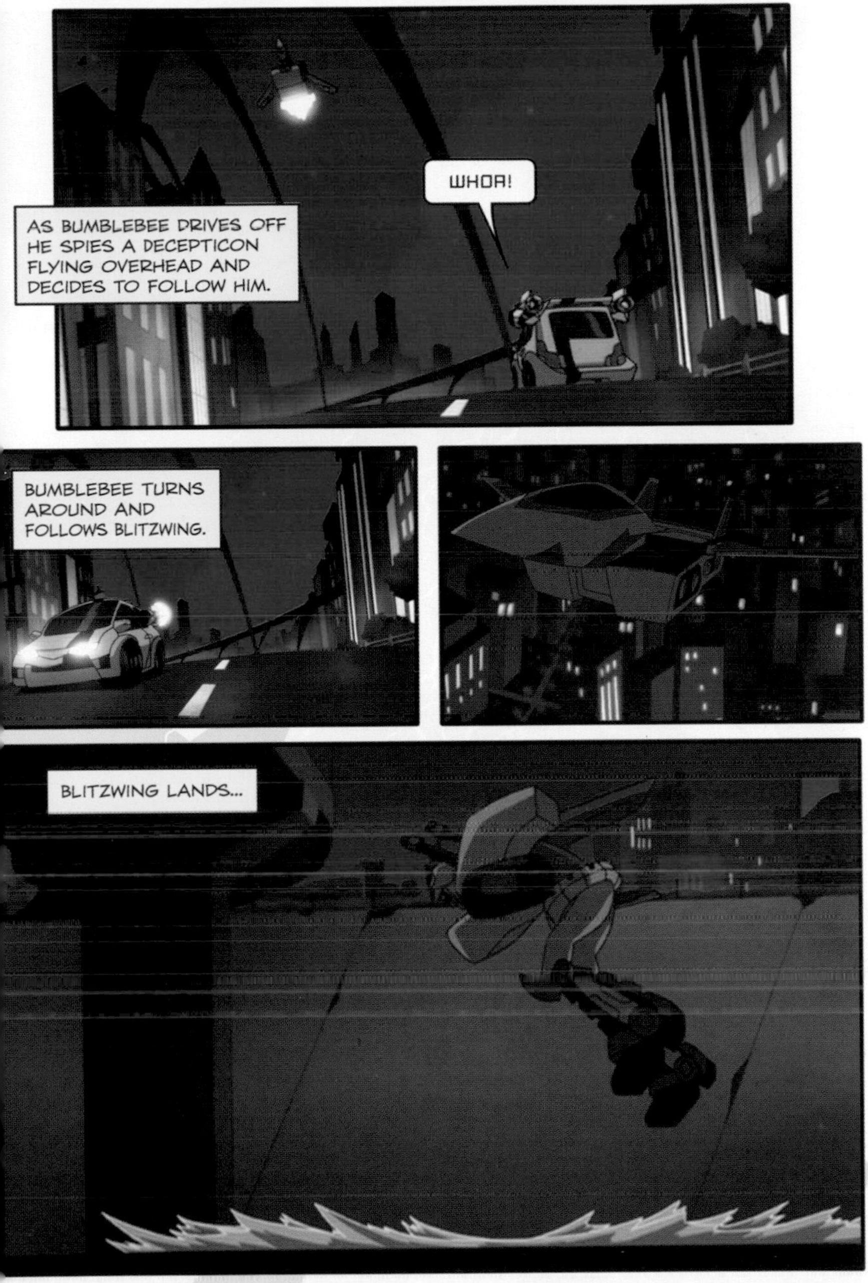
AS BUMBLEBEE DRIVES OFF HE SPIES A DECEPTICON FLYING OVERHEAD AND DECIDES TO FOLLOW HIM.
WHOA!
BUMBLEBEE TURNS AROUND AND FOLLOWS BLITZWING.
BLITZWING LANDS...

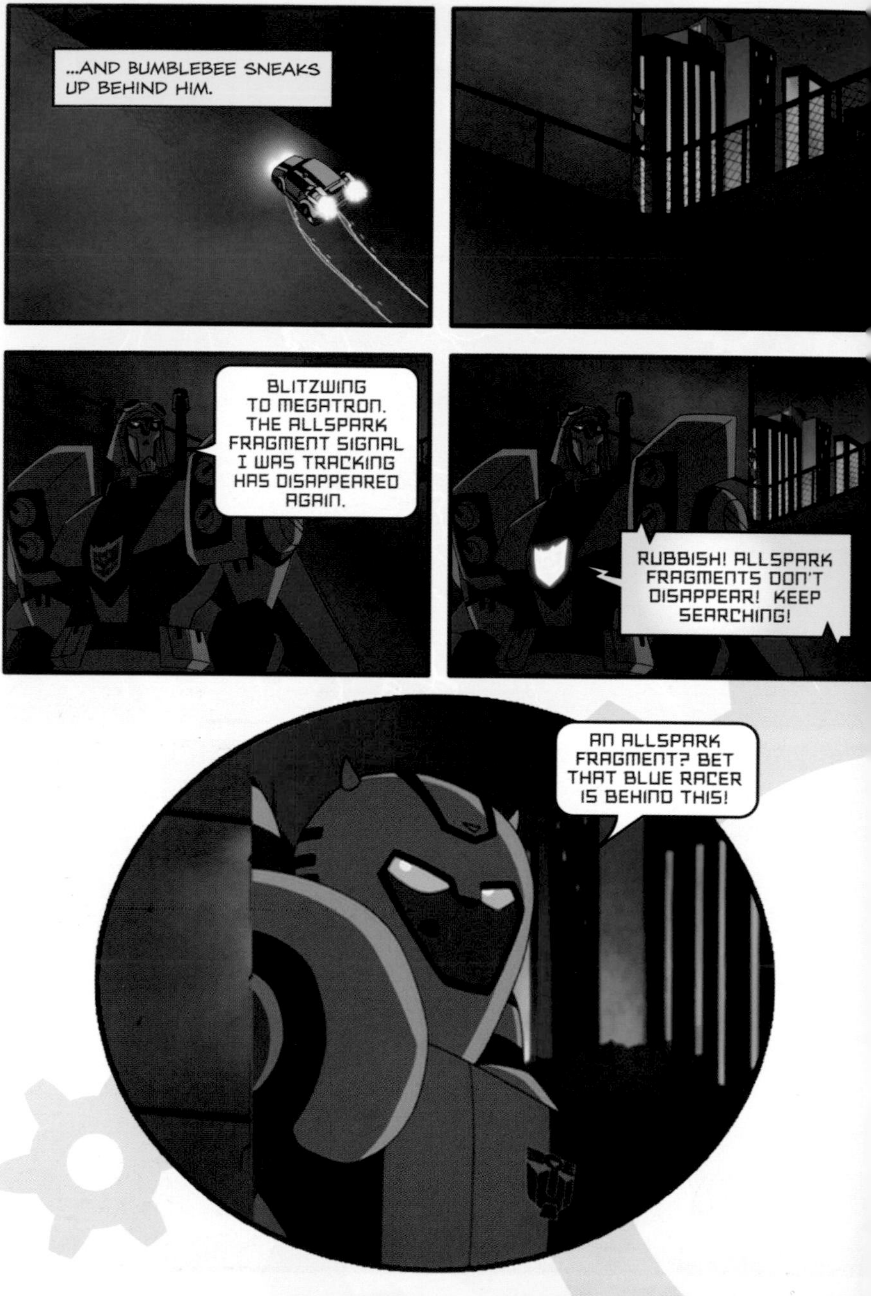
...AND BUMBLEBEE SNEAKS UP BEHIND HIM.
BLITZWING TO MEGATRON. THE ALLSPARK FRAGMENT SIGNAL I WAS TRACKING HAS DISAPPEARED AGAIN.
RUBBISH! ALLSPARK FRAGMENTS DON'T DISAPPEAR! KEEP SEARCHING!
AN ALLSPARK FRAGMENT? BET THAT BLUE RACER IS BEHIND THIS!

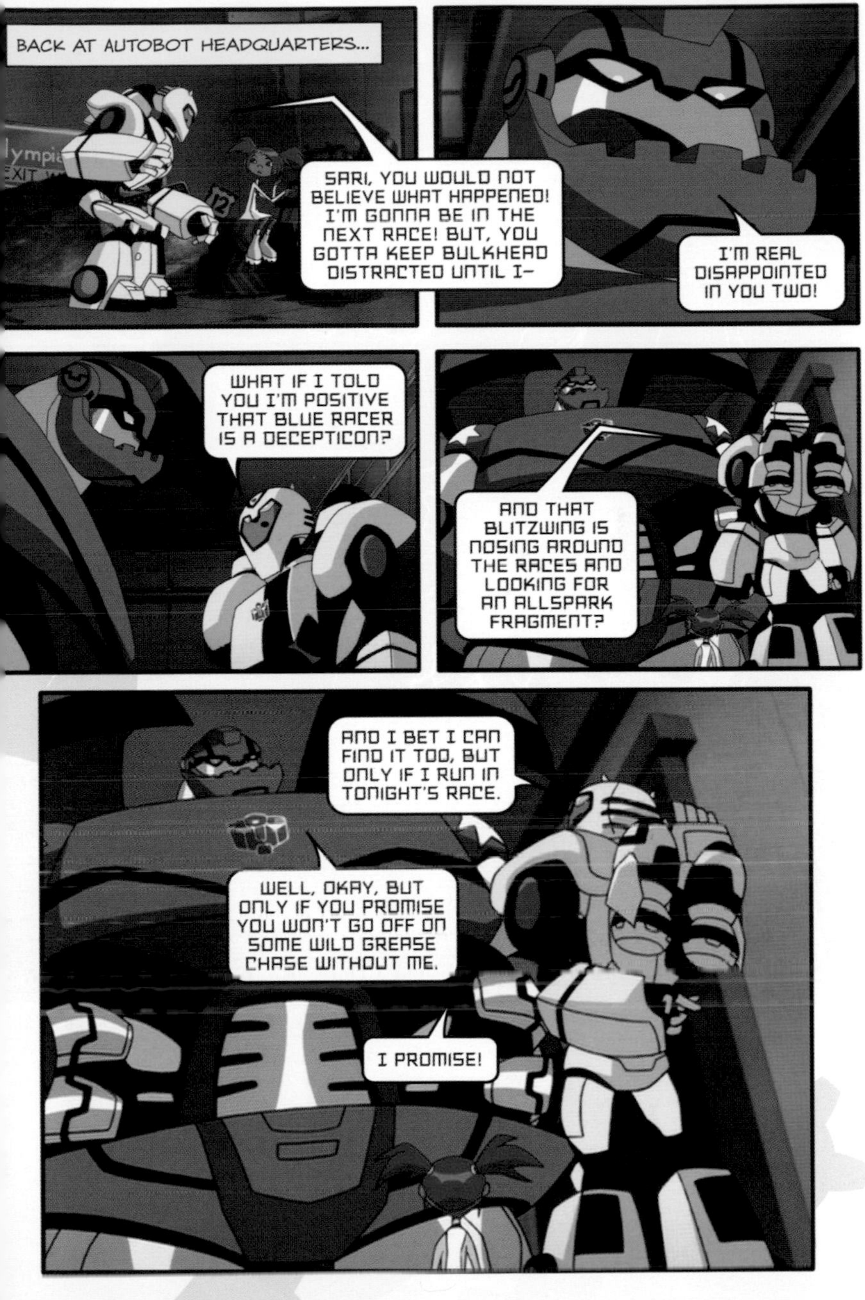
BACK AT AUTOBOT HEADQUARTERS...
SARI, YOU WOULD NOT BELIEVE WHAT HAPPENED! I'M GONNA BE IN THE NEXT RACE! BUT, YOU GOTTA KEEP BULKHEAD DISTRACTED UNTIL I–
I'M REAL DISAPPOINTED IN YOU TWO!
WHAT IF I TOLD YOU I'M POSITIVE THAT BLUE RACER IS A DECEPTICON?
AND THAT BLITZWING IS NOSING AROUND THE RACES AND LOOKING FOR AN ALLSPARK FRAGMENT?
AND I BET I CAN FIND IT TOO, BUT ONLY IF I RUN IN TONIGHT'S RACE.
WELL, OKAY, BUT ONLY IF YOU PROMISE YOU WON'T GO OFF ON SOME WILD GREASE CHASE WITHOUT ME.
I PROMISE!

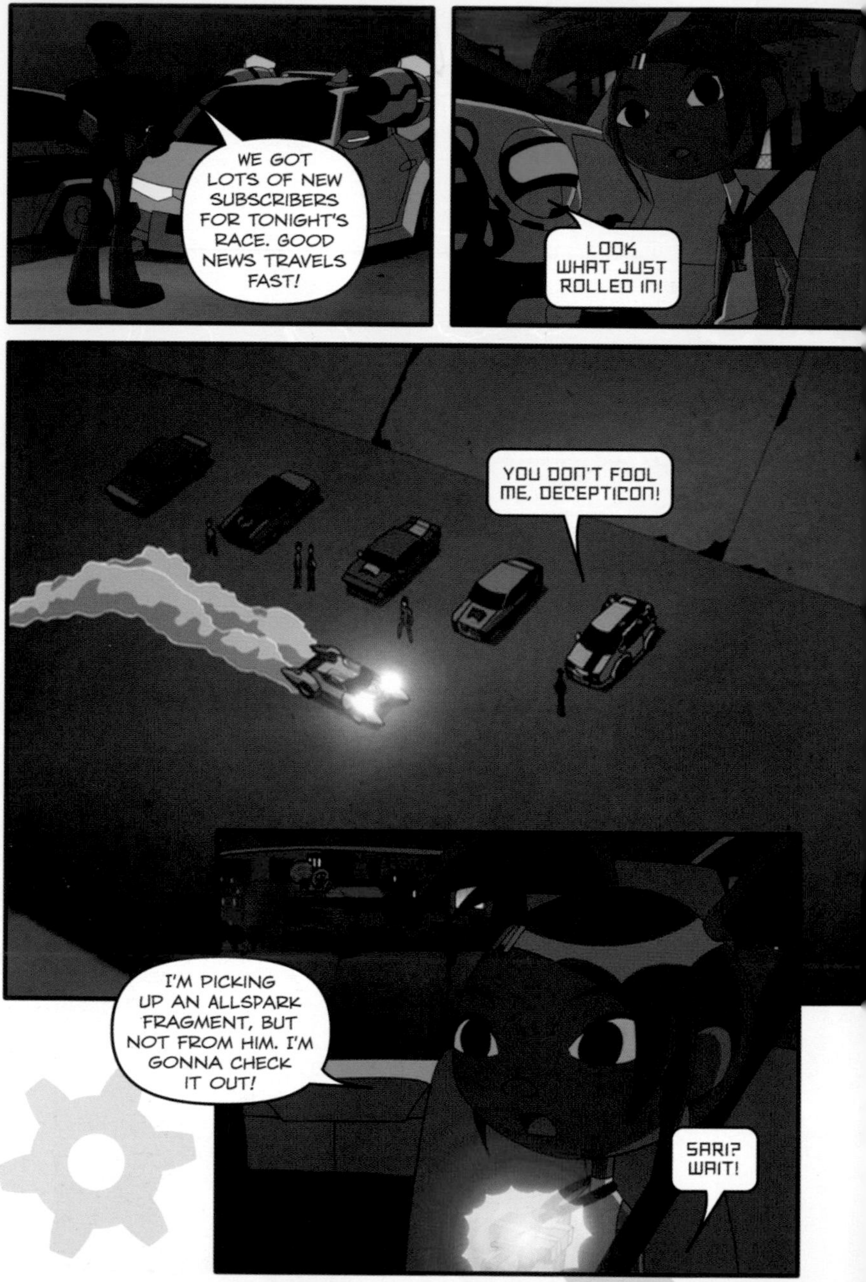
WE GOT LOTS OF NEW SUBSCRIBERS FOR TONIGHT'S RACE. GOOD NEWS TRAVELS FAST!
LOOK WHAT JUST ROLLED IN!
YOU DON'T FOOL ME, DECEPTICON!
I'M PICKING UP AN ALLSPARK FRAGMENT, BUT NOT FROM HIM. I'M GONNA CHECK IT OUT!
SARI? WAIT!

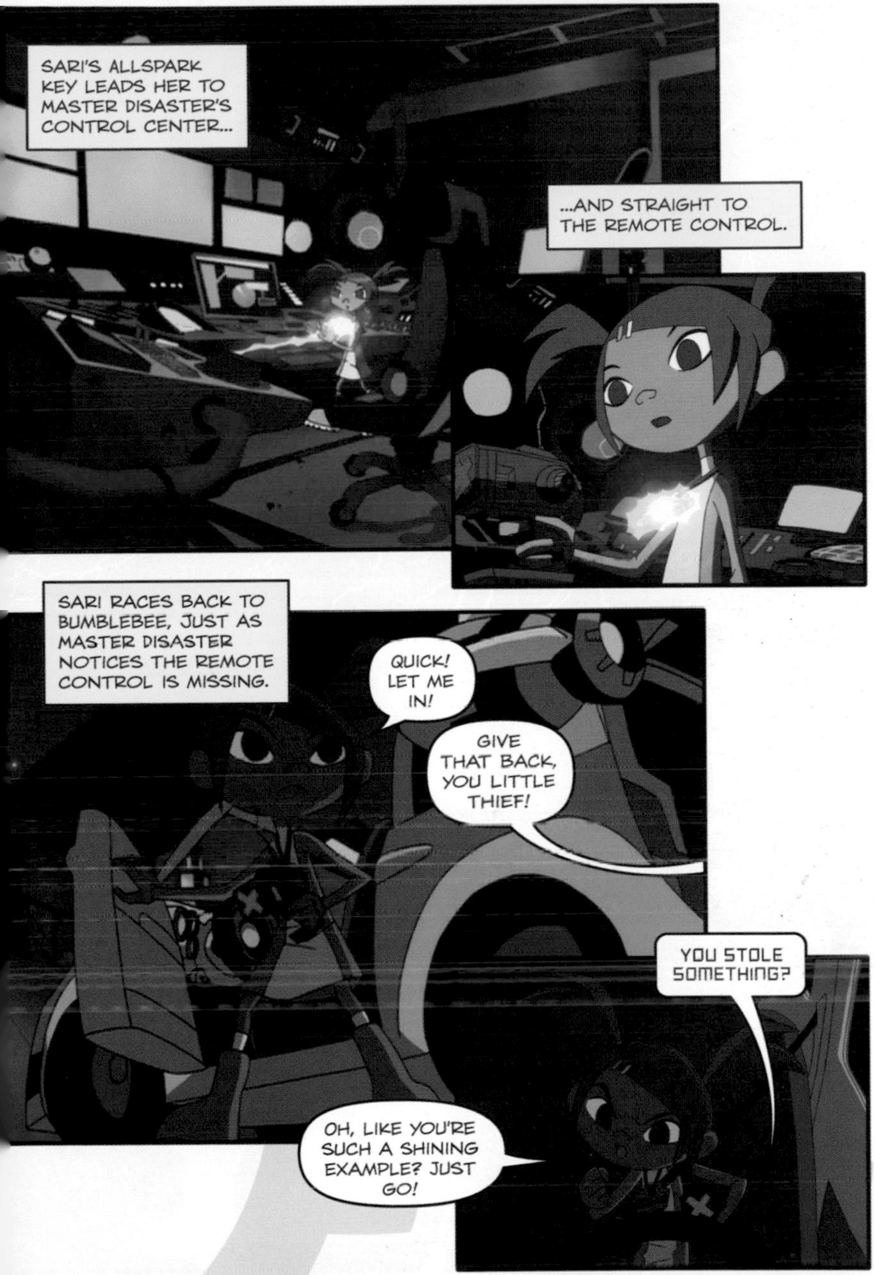
SARI'S ALLSPARK KEY LEADS HER TO MASTER DISASTER'S CONTROL CENTER...
...AND STRAIGHT TO THE REMOTE CONTROL.
SARI RACES BACK TO BUMBLEBEE, JUST AS MASTER DISASTER NOTICES THE REMOTE CONTROL IS MISSING.
QUICK! LET ME IN!
GIVE THAT BACK, YOU LITTLE THIEF!
YOU STOLE SOMETHING?
OH, LIKE YOU'RE SUCH A SHINING EXAMPLE? JUST GO!

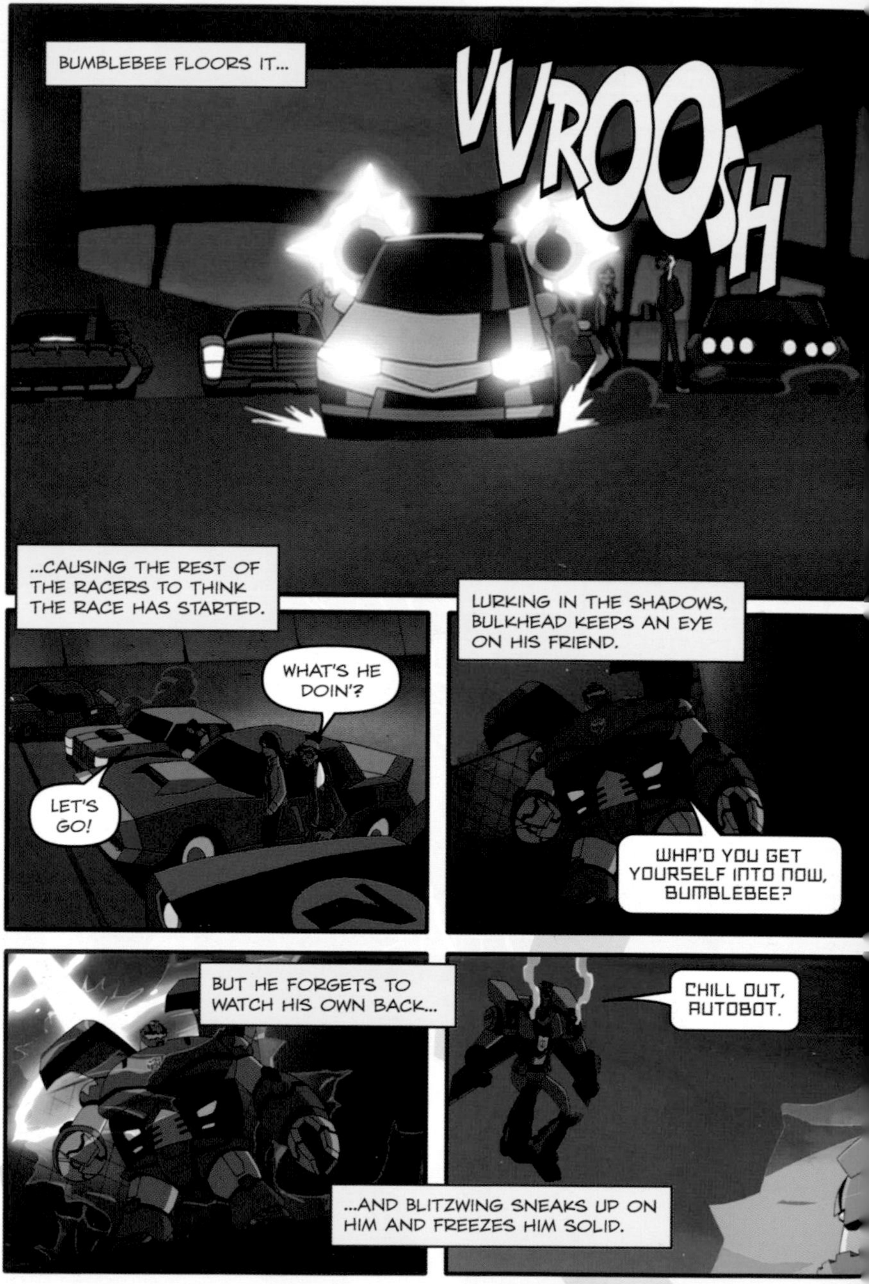

BUMBLEBEE FLOORS IT...
VVROOSH
...CAUSING THE REST OF THE RACERS TO THINK THE RACE HAS STARTED.
WHAT'S HE DOIN'?
LET'S GO!
LURKING IN THE SHADOWS, BULKHEAD KEEPS AN EYE ON HIS FRIEND.
WHA'D YOU GET YOURSELF INTO NOW, BUMBLEBEE?
BUT HE FORGETS TO WATCH HIS OWN BACK...
CHILL OUT, AUTOBOT.
...AND BLITZWING SNEAKS UP ON HIM AND FREEZES HIM SOLID.

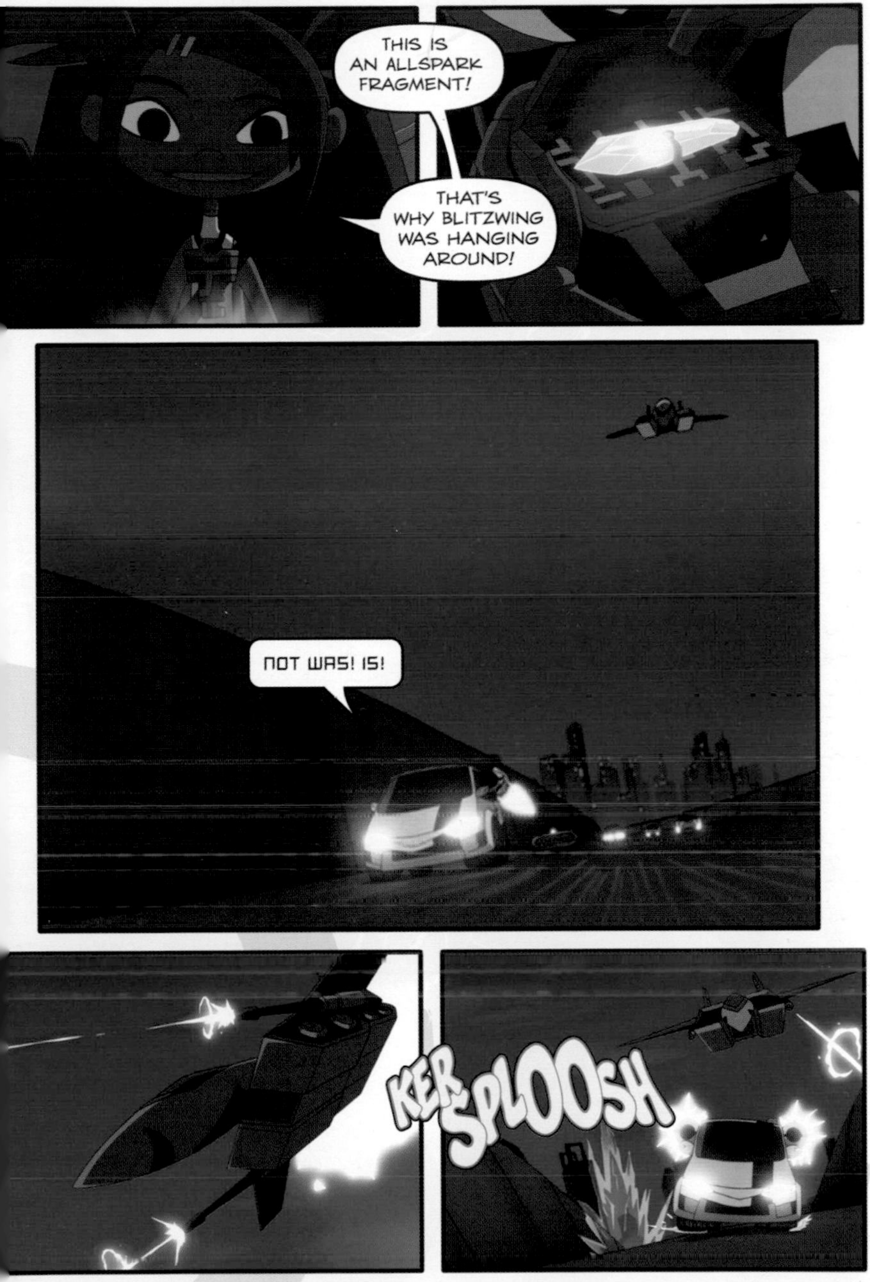
THIS IS AN ALLSPARK FRAGMENT!
THAT'S WHY BLITZWING WAS HANGING AROUND!
NOT WAS! IS!
KERSPLOOSH

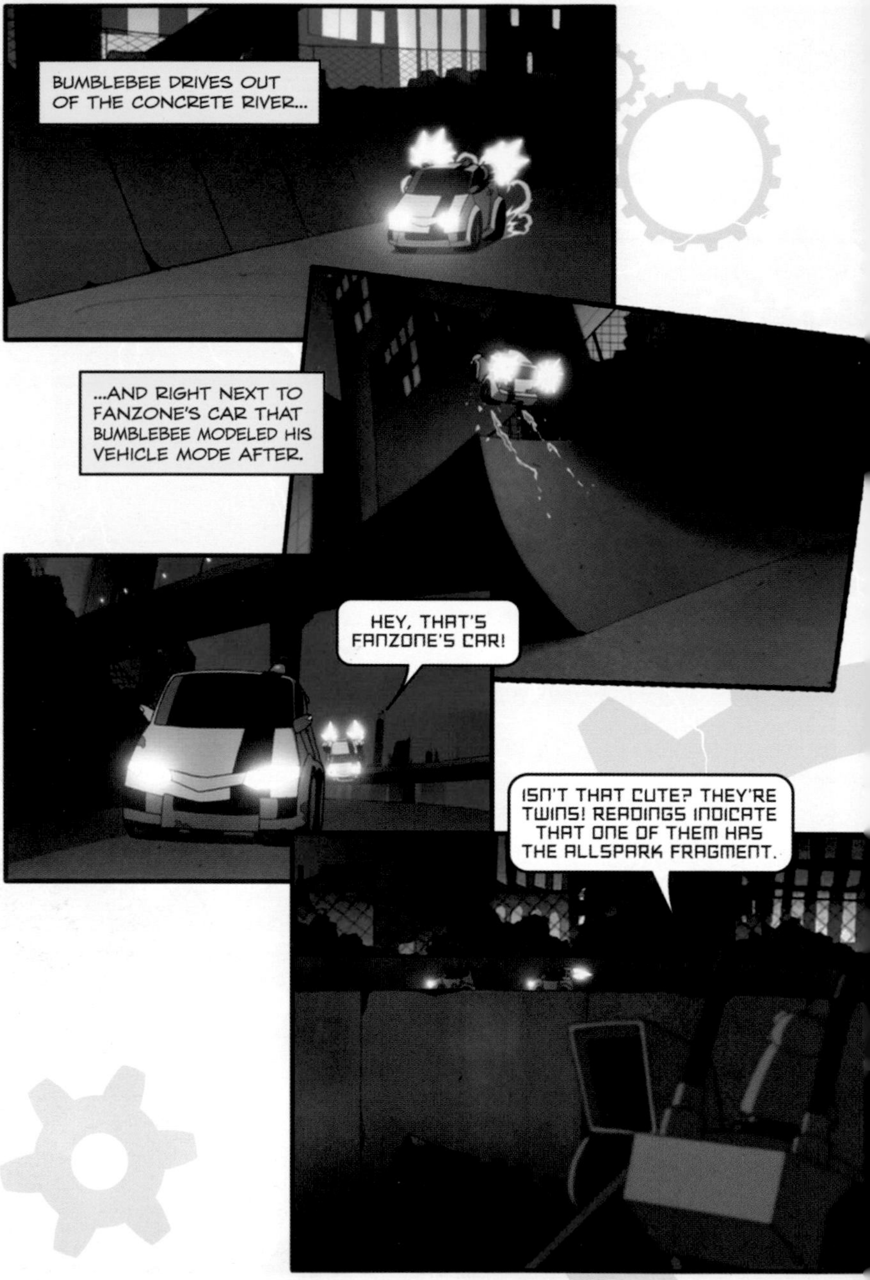
BUMBLEBEE DRIVES OUT OF THE CONCRETE RIVER...
...AND RIGHT NEXT TO FANZONE'S CAR THAT BUMBLEBEE MODELED HIS VEHICLE MODE AFTER.
HEY, THAT'S FANZONE'S CAR!
ISN'T THAT CUTE? THEY'RE TWINS! READINGS INDICATE THAT ONE OF THEM HAS THE ALLSPARK FRAGMENT.

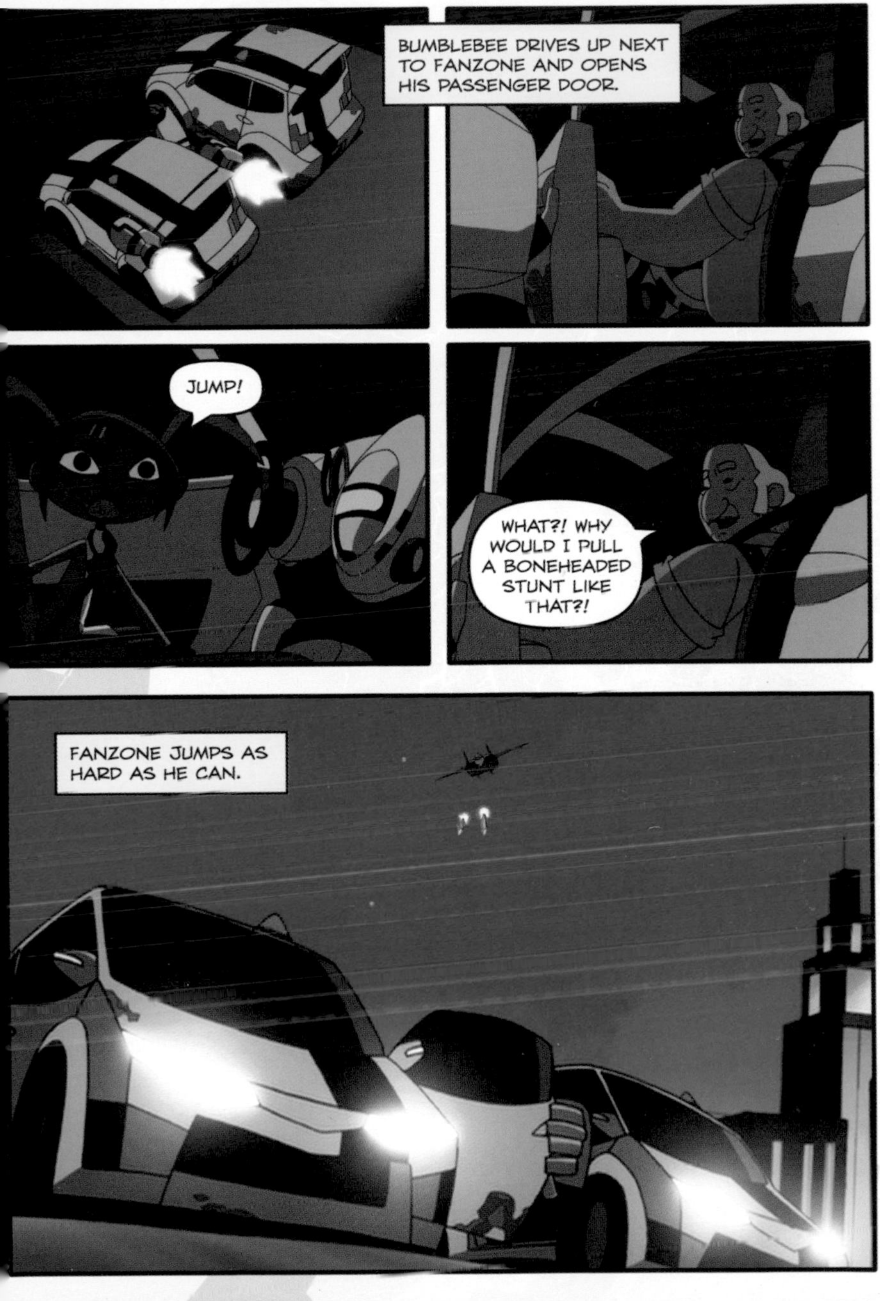
BUMBLEBEE DRIVES UP NEXT TO FANZONE AND OPENS HIS PASSENGER DOOR.
JUMP!
WHAT?! WHY WOULD I PULL A BONEHEADED STUNT LIKE THAT?!
FANZONE JUMPS AS HARD AS HE CAN.

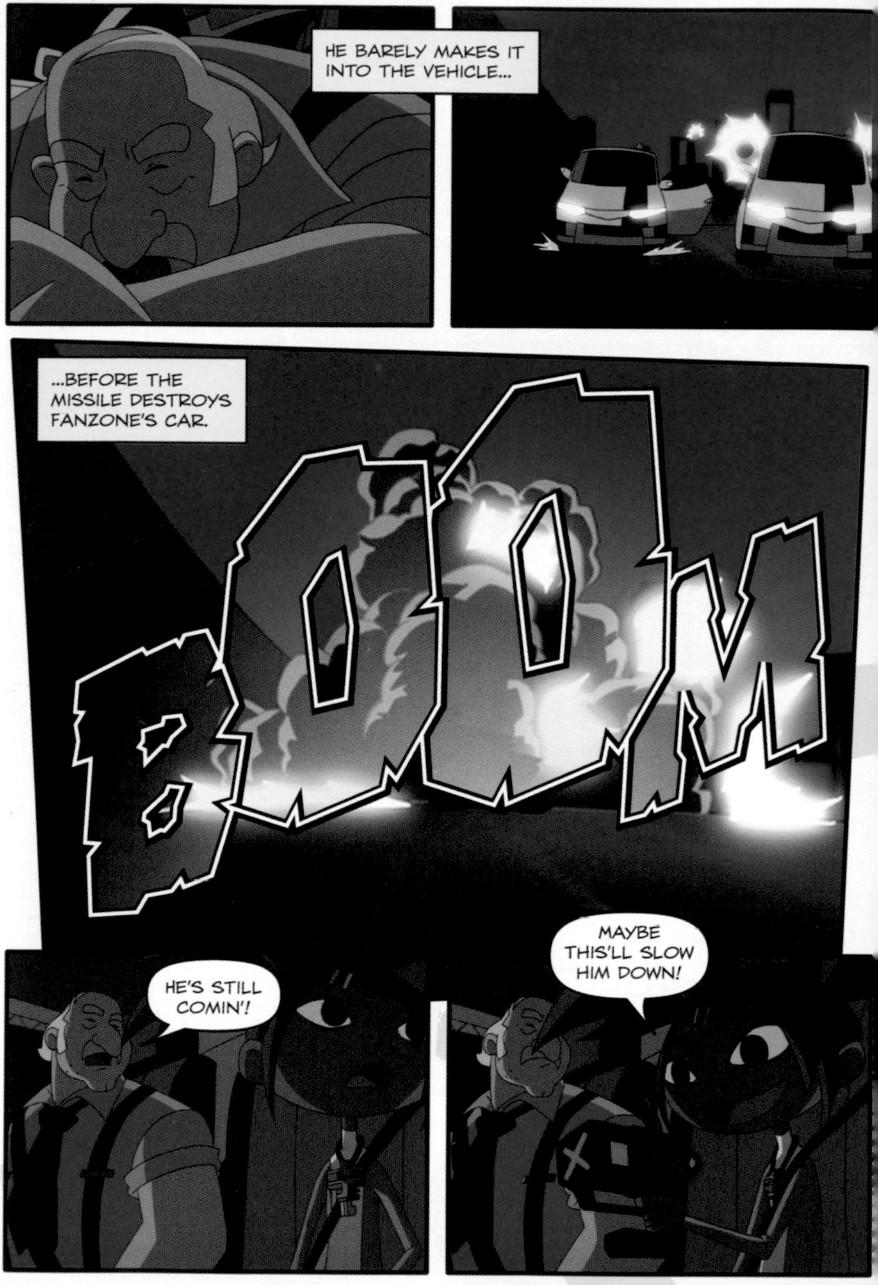
HE BARELY MAKES IT INTO THE VEHICLE...
...BEFORE THE MISSILE DESTROYS FANZONE'S CAR.
BOOM
HE'S STILL COMIN'!
MAYBE THIS'LL SLOW HIM DOWN!

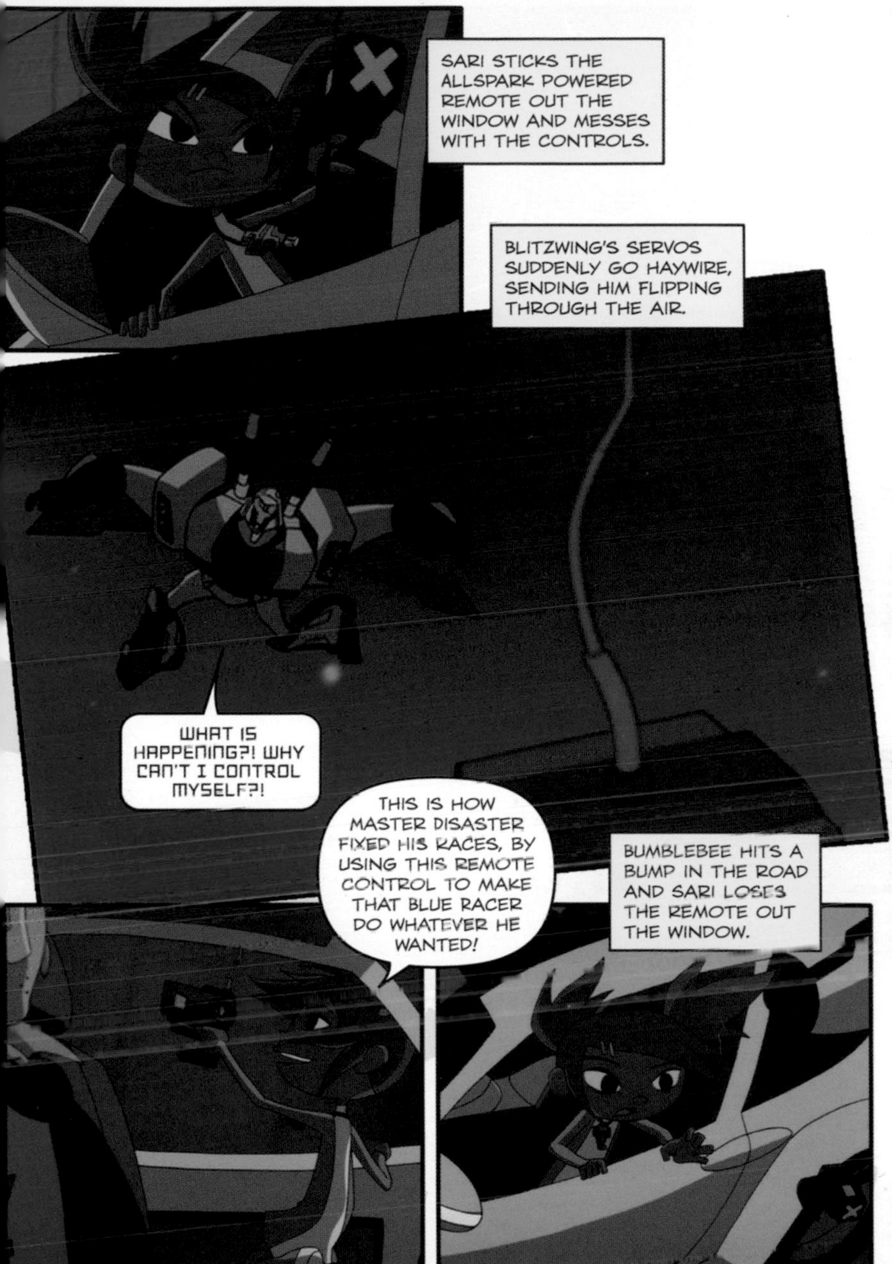
SARI STICKS THE ALLSPARK POWERED REMOTE OUT THE WINDOW AND MESSES WITH THE CONTROLS.
BLITZWING'S SERVOS SUDDENLY GO HAYWIRE, SENDING HIM FLIPPING THROUGH THE AIR.
WHAT IS HAPPENING?! WHY CAN'T I CONTROL MYSELF?!
THIS IS HOW MASTER DISASTER FIXED HIS RACES, BY USING THIS REMOTE CONTROL TO MAKE THAT BLUE RACER DO WHATEVER HE WANTED!
BUMBLEBEE HITS A BUMP IN THE ROAD AND SARI LOSES THE REMOTE OUT THE WINDOW.

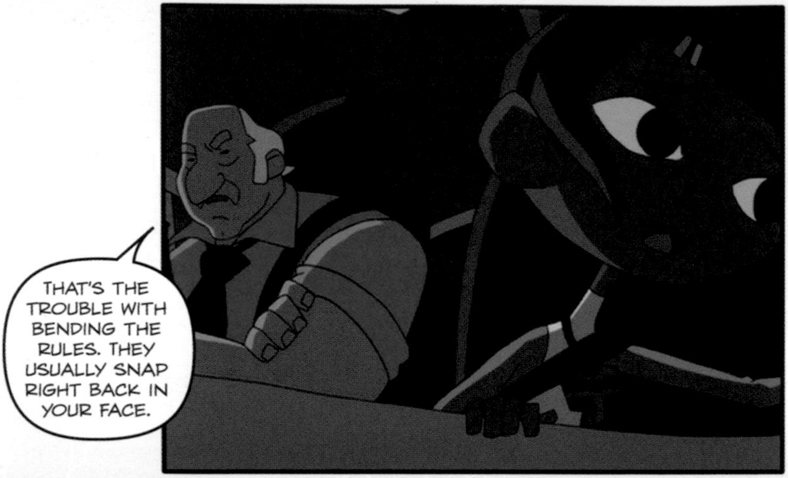
THAT'S THE TROUBLE WITH BENDING THE RULES. THEY USUALLY SNAP RIGHT BACK IN YOUR FACE.

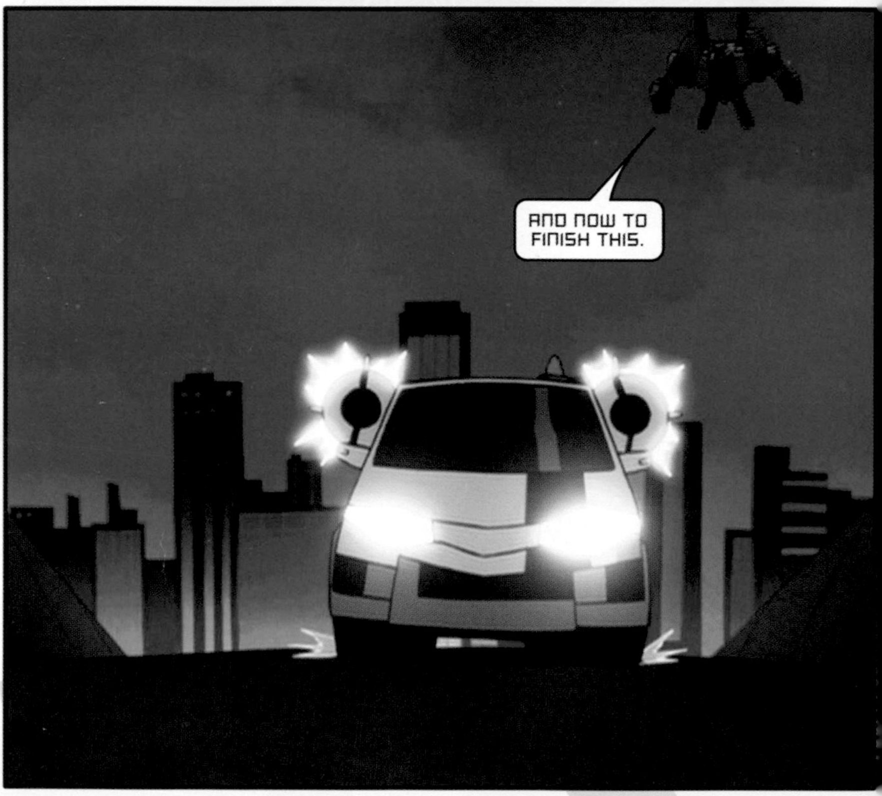
AND NOW TO FINISH THIS.

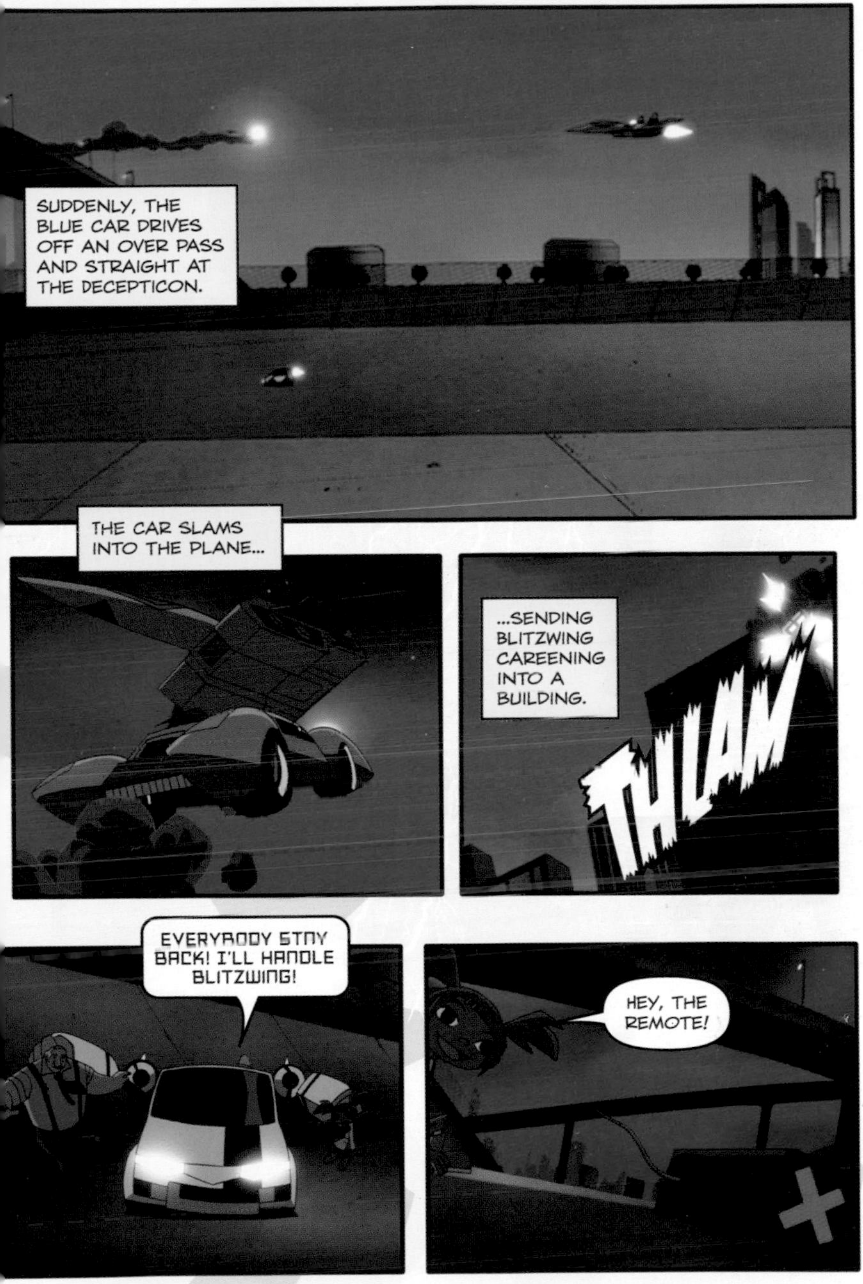
SUDDENLY, THE BLUE CAR DRIVES OFF AN OVER PASS AND STRAIGHT AT THE DECEPTICON.
THE CAR SLAMS INTO THE PLANE...
...SENDING BLITZWING CAREENING INTO A BUILDING.
THLAM
EVERYBODY STAY BACK! I'LL HANDLE BLITZWING!
HEY, THE REMOTE!

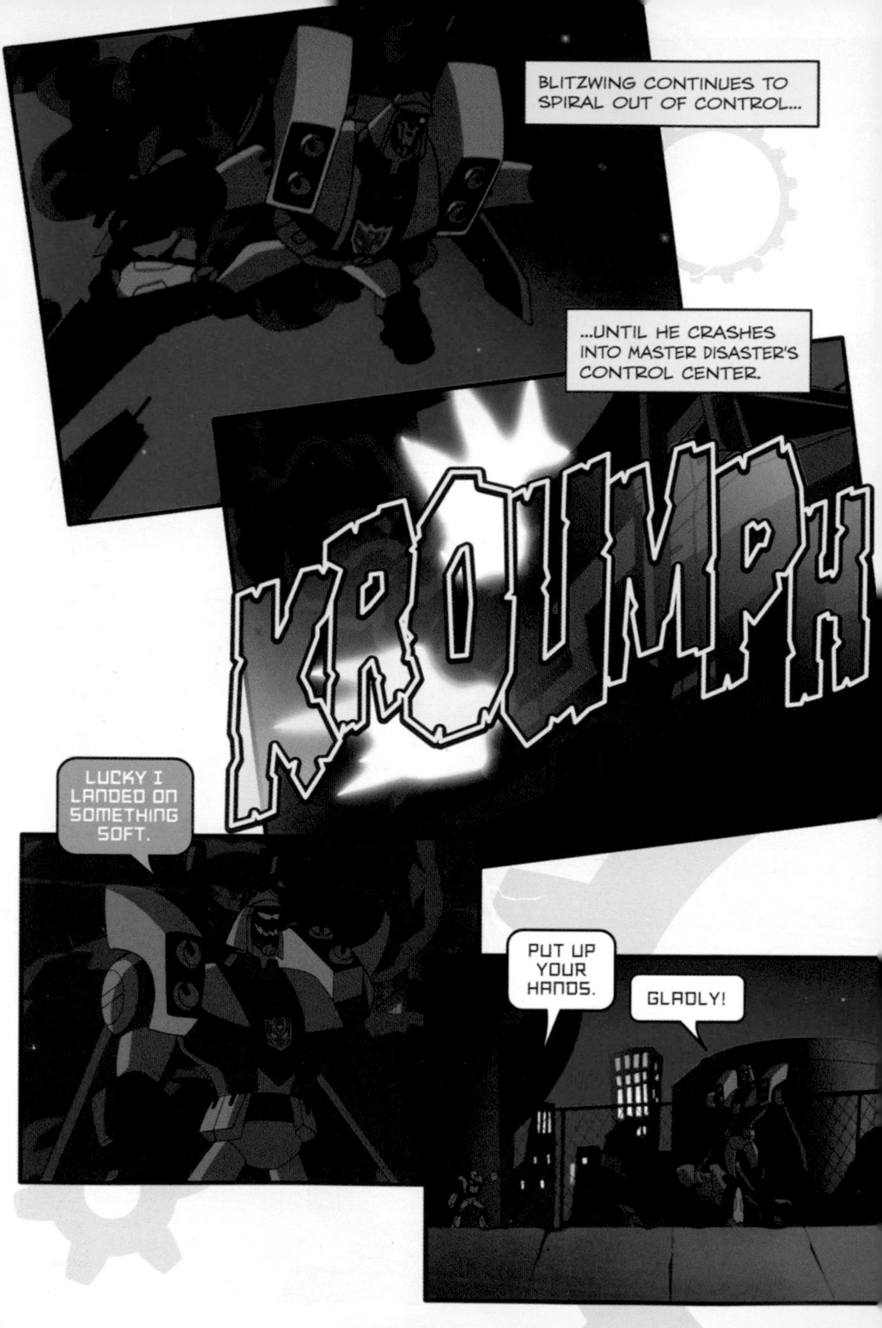
BLITZWING CONTINUES TO SPIRAL OUT OF CONTROL...
...UNTIL HE CRASHES INTO MASTER DISASTER'S CONTROL CENTER.
KROUMPH
LUCKY I LANDED ON SOMETHING SOFT.
PUT UP YOUR HANDS.
GLADLY!

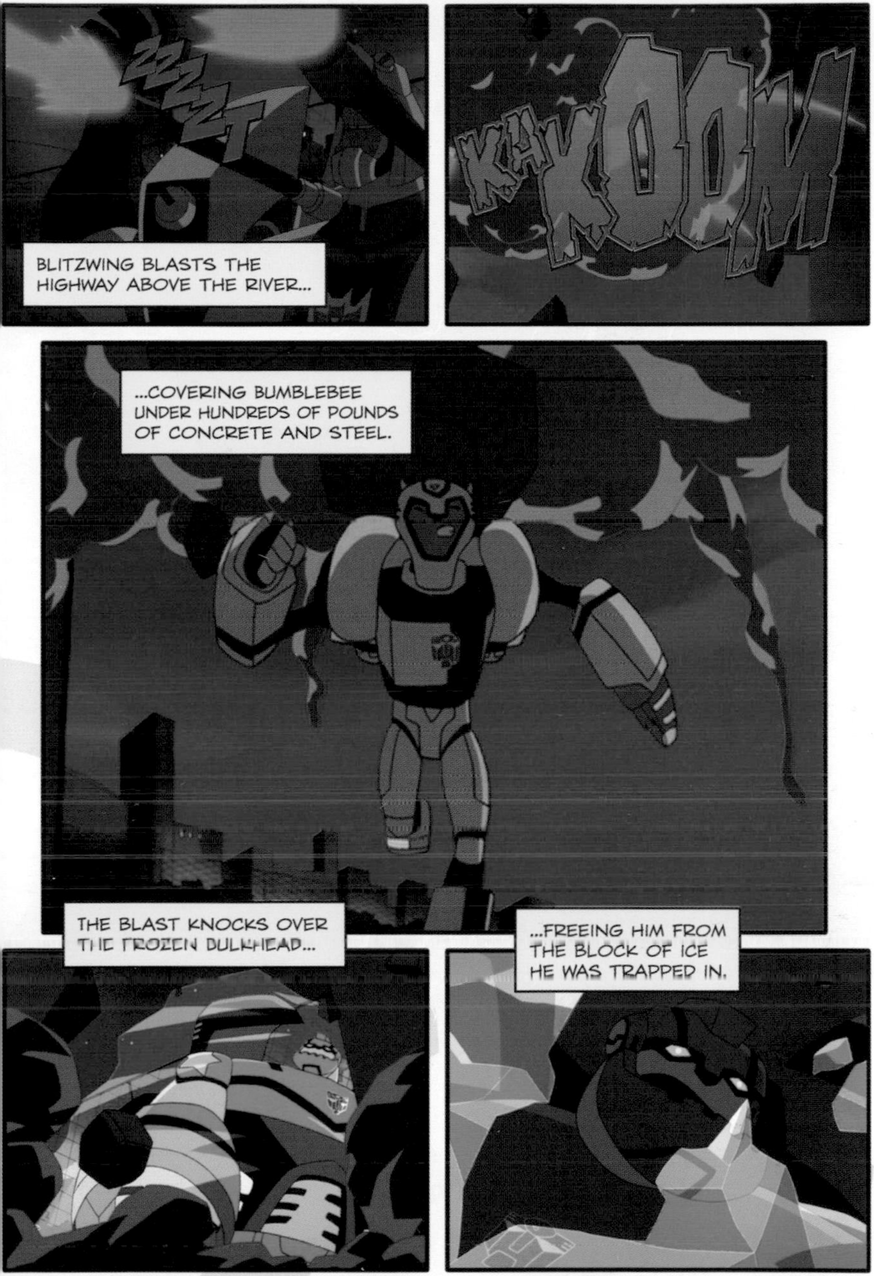
ZZZZZT
BLITZWING BLASTS THE HIGHWAY ABOVE THE RIVER...
KAHKOOM
...COVERING BUMBLEBEE UNDER HUNDREDS OF POUNDS OF CONCRETE AND STEEL.
THE BLAST KNOCKS OVER THE FROZEN BULKHEAD...
...FREEING HIM FROM THE BLOCK OF ICE HE WAS TRAPPED IN.

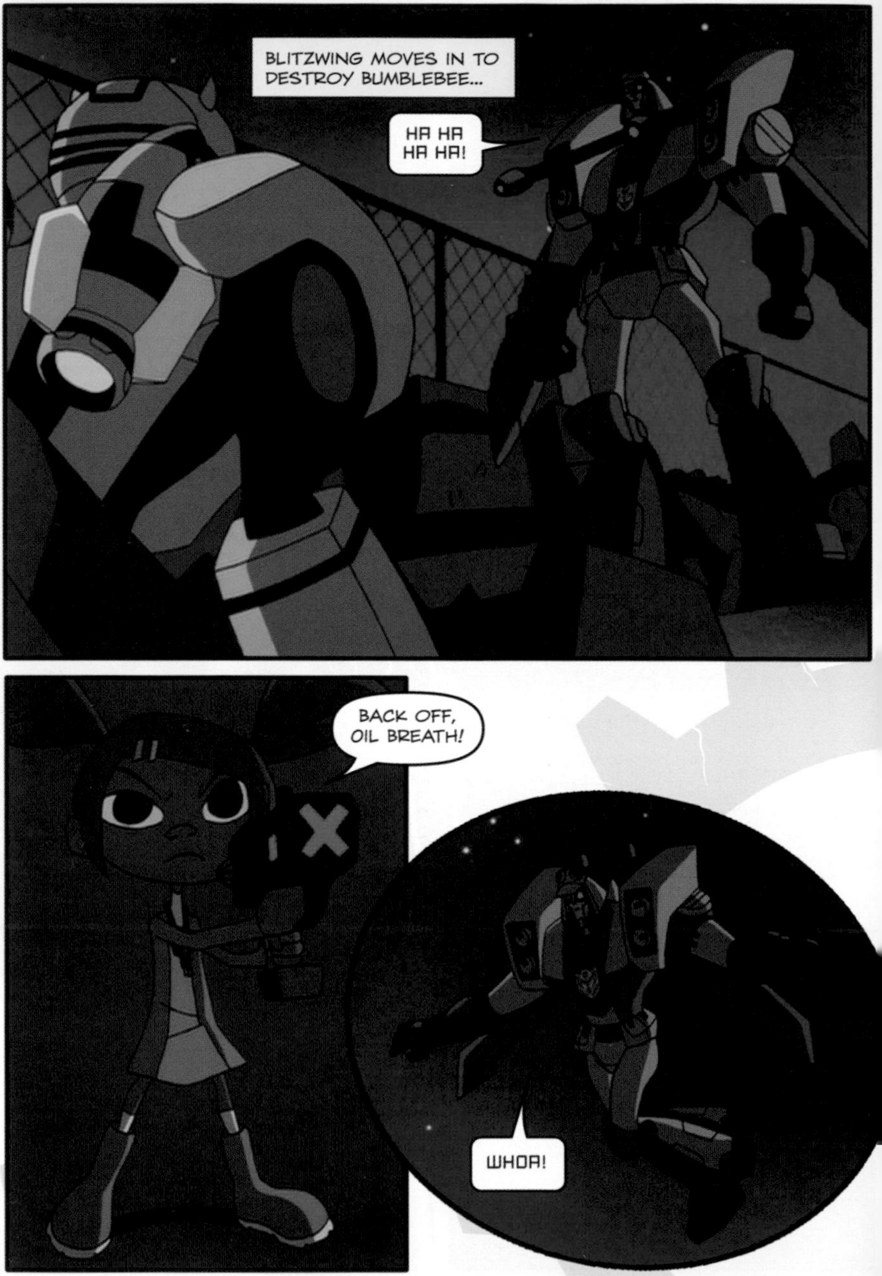
BLITZWING MOVES IN TO DESTROY BUMBLEBEE...
HA HA HA HA!
BACK OFF, OIL BREATH!
WHOA!

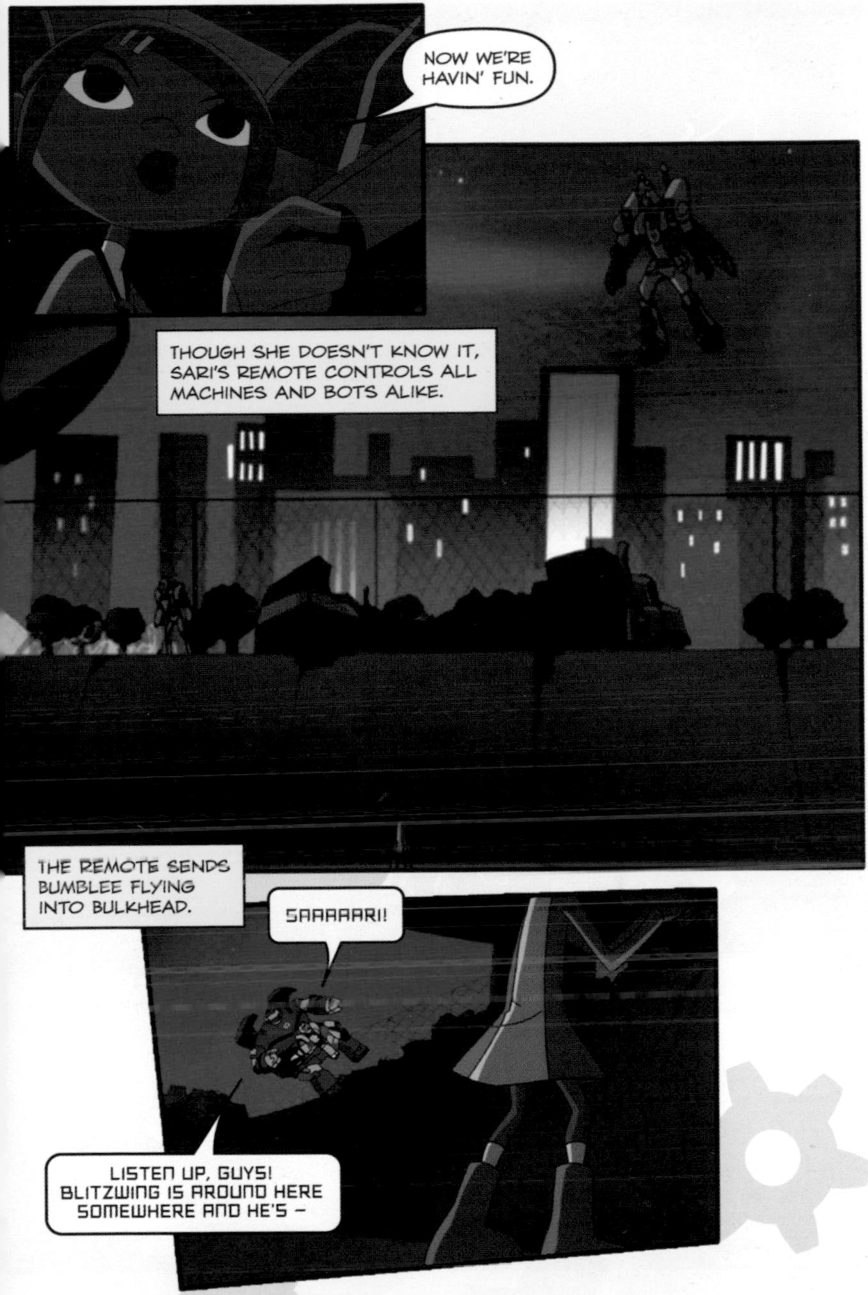
NOW WE'RE HAVIN' FUN.
THOUGH SHE DOESN'T KNOW IT, SARI'S REMOTE CONTROLS ALL MACHINES AND BOTS ALIKE.
THE REMOTE SENDS BUMBLEE FLYING INTO BULKHEAD.
SAAAAARI!
LISTEN UP, GUYS! BLITZWING IS AROUND HERE SOMEWHERE AND HE'S –

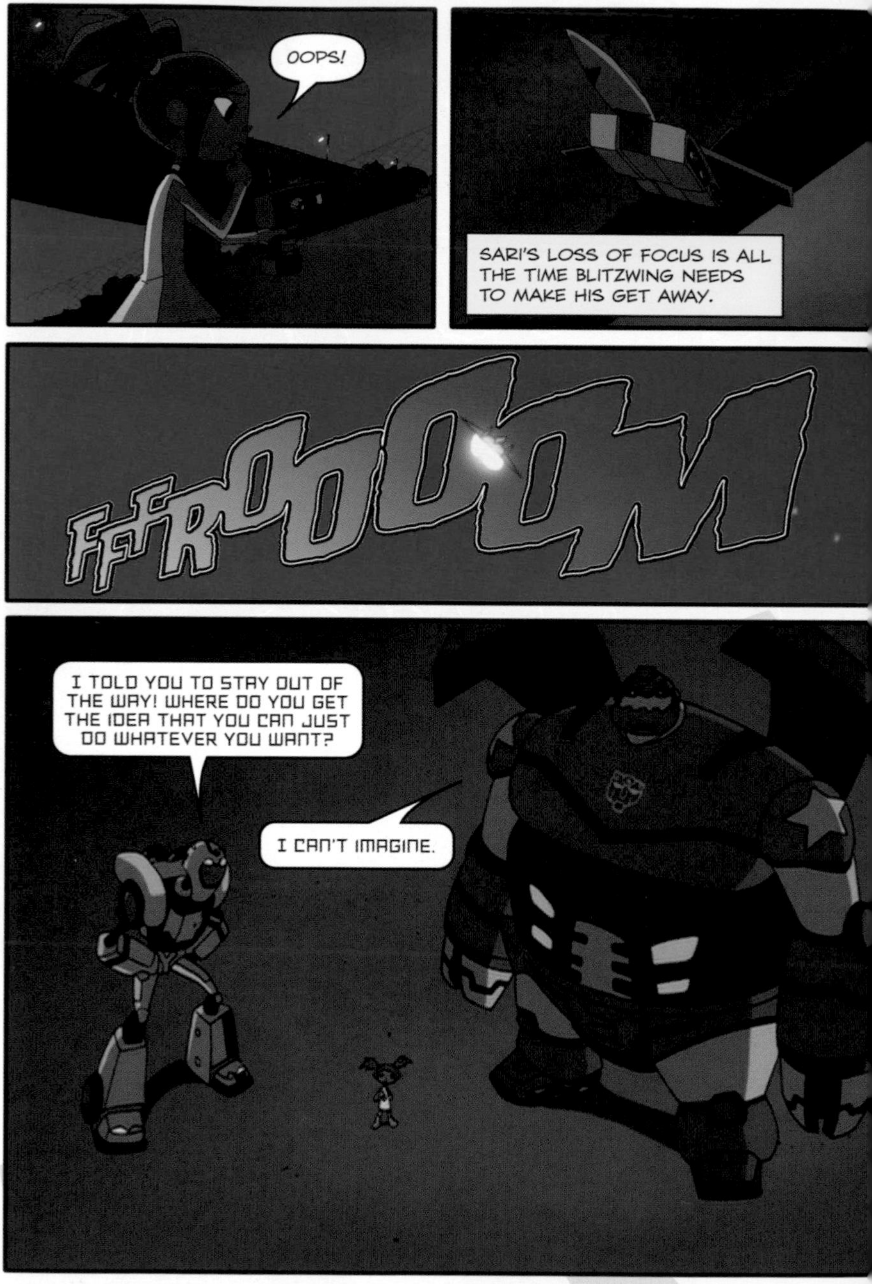
OOPS!
SARI'S LOSS OF FOCUS IS ALL THE TIME BLITZWING NEEDS TO MAKE HIS GET AWAY.
FFFROOOOM
I TOLD YOU TO STAY OUT OF THE WAY! WHERE DO YOU GET THE IDEA THAT YOU CAN JUST DO WHATEVER YOU WANT?
I CAN'T IMAGINE.

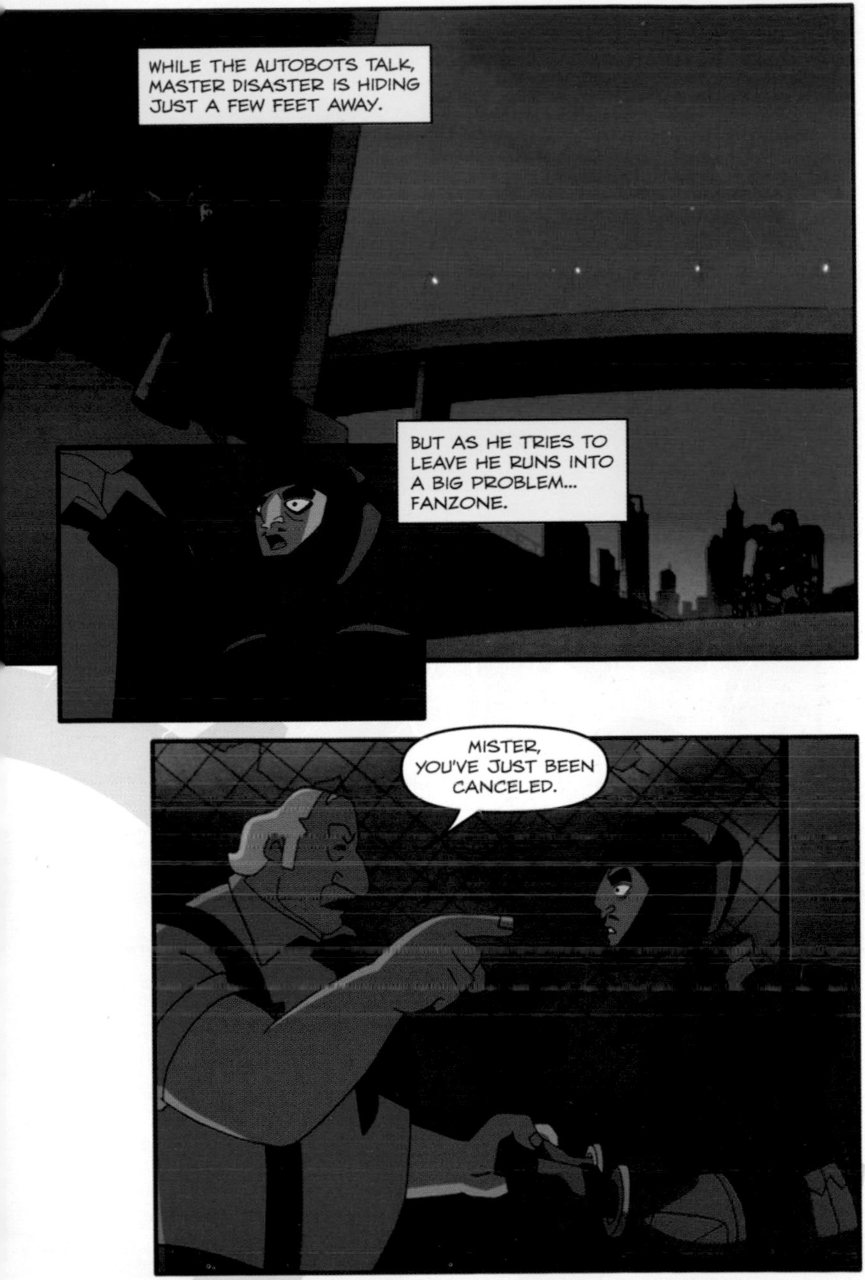
WHILE THE AUTOBOTS TALK, MASTER DISASTER IS HIDING JUST A FEW FEET AWAY.
BUT AS HE TRIES TO LEAVE HE RUNS INTO A BIG PROBLEM... FANZONE.
MISTER, YOU'VE JUST BEEN CANCELED.

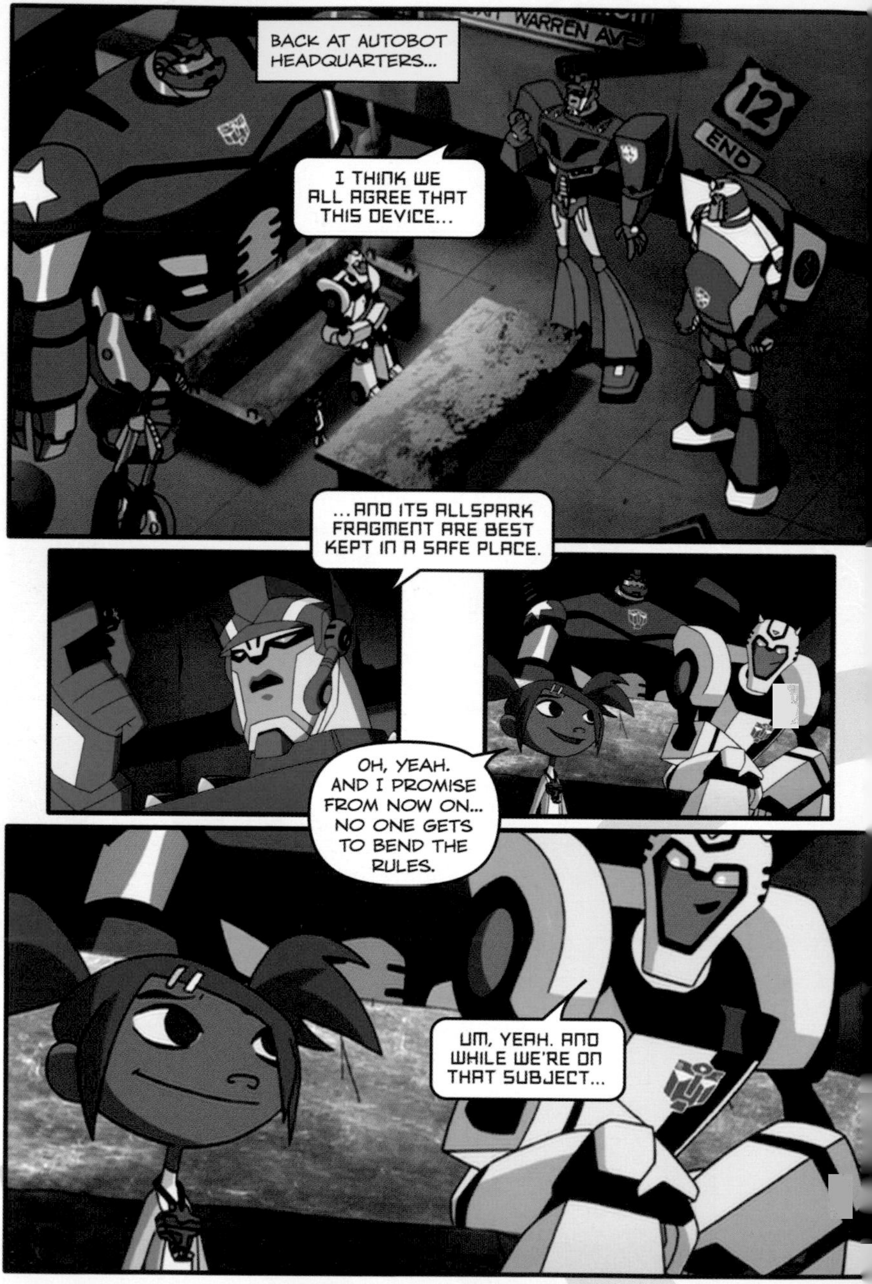
WARREN AVE
BACK AT AUTOBOT HEADQUARTERS...
12
END
I THINK WE ALL AGREE THAT THIS DEVICE...
...AND ITS ALLSPARK FRAGMENT ARE BEST KEPT IN A SAFE PLACE.
OH, YEAH. AND I PROMISE FROM NOW ON... NO ONE GETS TO BEND THE RULES.
UM, YEAH. AND WHILE WE'RE ON THAT SUBJECT...

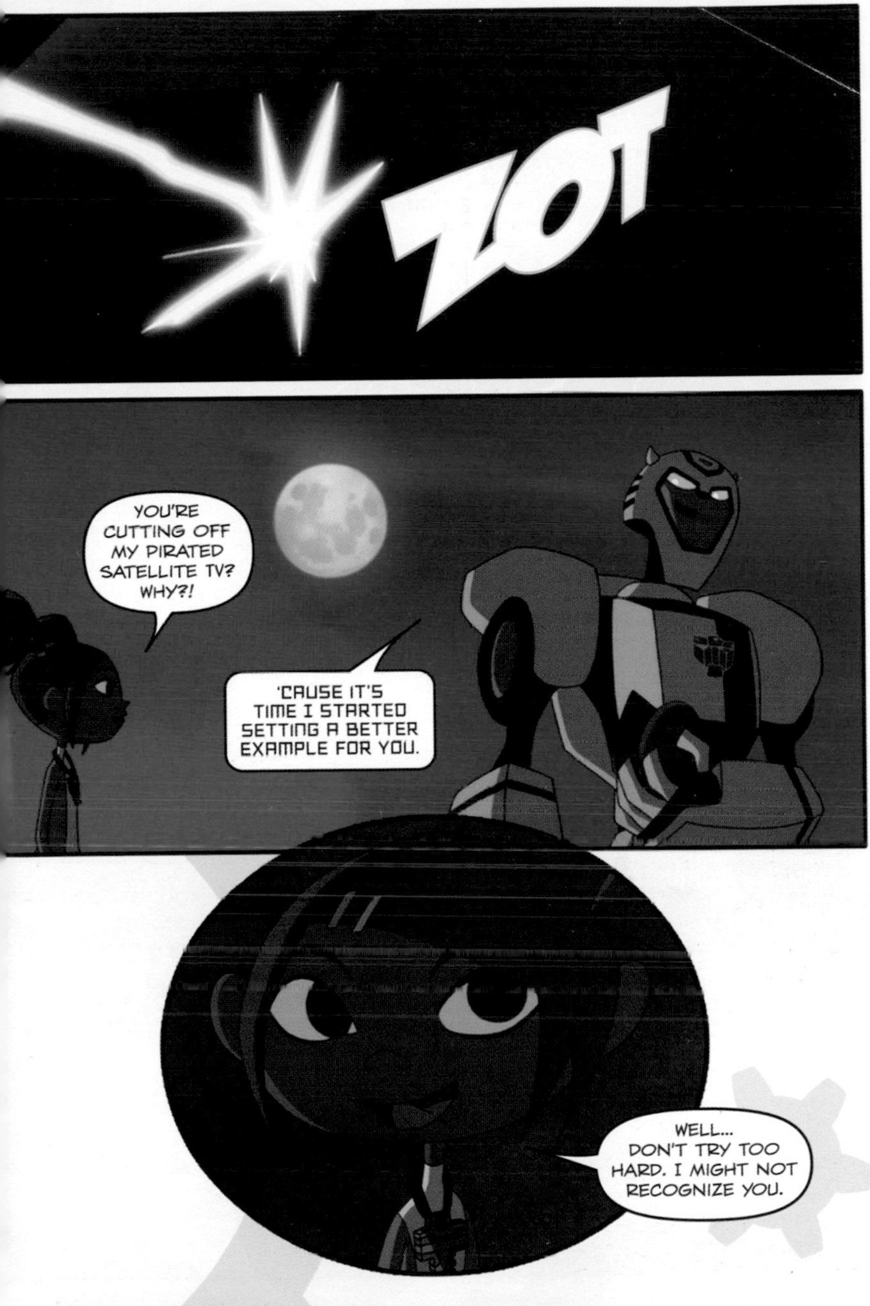
ZOT
YOU'RE CUTTING OFF MY PIRATED SATELLITE TV? WHY?!
'CAUSE IT'S TIME I STARTED SETTING A BETTER EXAMPLE FOR YOU.
WELL... DON'T TRY TOO HARD. I MIGHT NOT RECOGNIZE YOU.

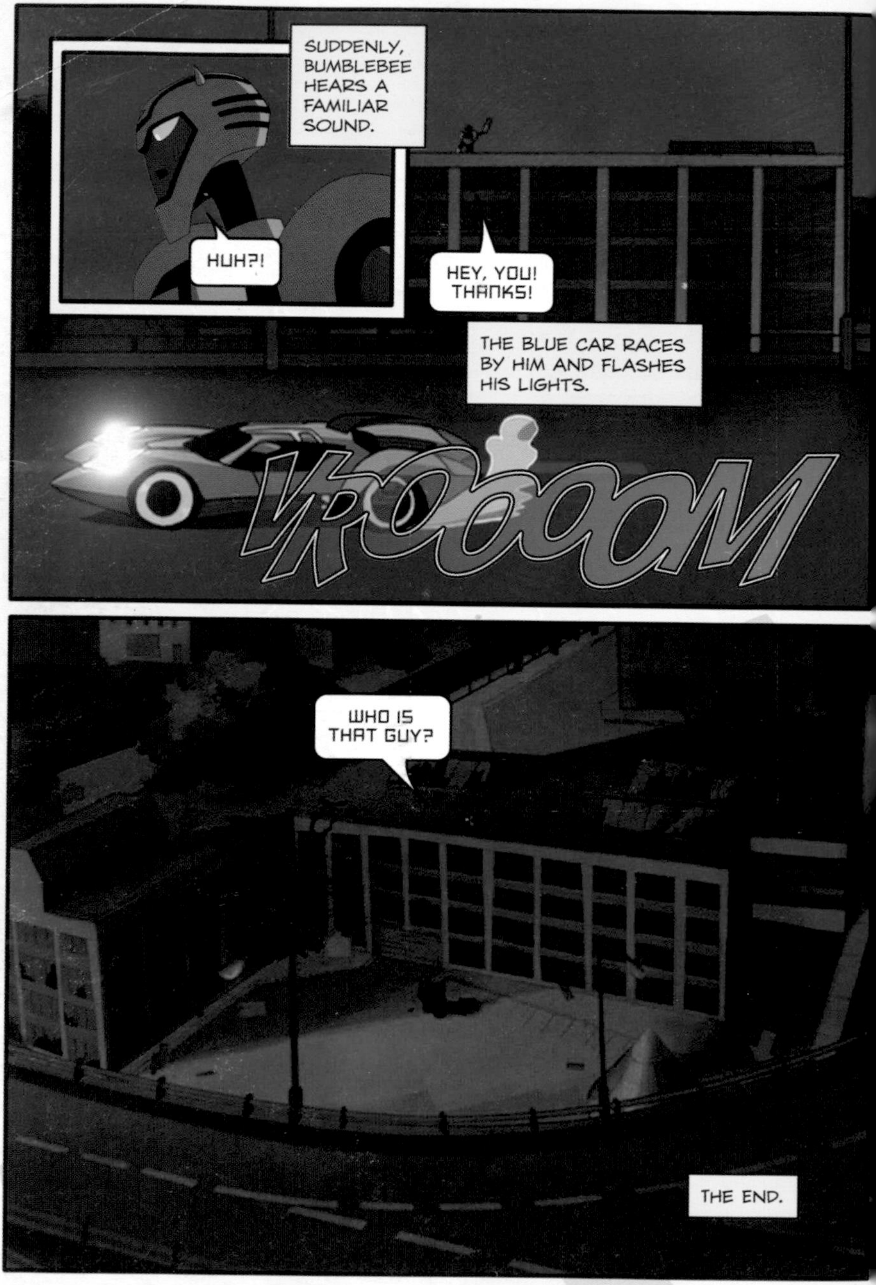
SUDDENLY, BUMBLEBEE HEARS A FAMILIAR SOUND.
HUH?!
HEY, YOU! THANKS!
THE BLUE CAR RACES BY HIM AND FLASHES HIS LIGHTS.
VROOOOM
WHO IS THAT GUY?
THE END.